SHAMROCK NURSE

Nurse Nuala Kavanagh, sent to nurse Blake Wendover after the surgeon's eyes have been accidentally damaged, is as concerned as the rest of St Jude's staff about his sight. Will she ever be more than a softly-voiced, gentle presence to him?

SHAMROCK NURSE

BY
ELSPETH O'BRIEN

MILLS & BOON LIMITED
London · Sydney · Toronto

First published in Great Britain 1983
by Mills & Boon Limited, 15–16 Brook's Mews,
London W1A 1DR

ISBN 0 263 74324 1

40,654

Set in 11 on 11½ pt Linotron Times
03/0783

Photoset by Rowland Phototypesetting Ltd
Bury St Edmunds, Suffolk
Made and printed in Great Britain by
Richard Clay (The Chaucer Press) Ltd
Bungay, Suffolk

CHAPTER ONE

NURSE Nuala Kavanagh sighed. St Jude's was the same as ever, even to the flaking paint on its walls near Outpatients and the potholes in the driveway that had nearly thrown her off her bicycle when she was training there. There had been times when she had walked the hard tiled corridors with laughter in her heart, one of a set of girls who shared the daily routine, the joys and hardships of all nurses starting their careers. But she might have known that it would be a mistake to come back to any place where happiness had gone hand in hand with a sense of vocation.

It's just me, she thought, with a shrug. I expected to see a few familiar faces and to pick up where I left off. But now there was nobody with whom she could share silly jokes, nobody who had known her during her training. She tweaked the staff nurse's cap impatiently. Once, it had been her ambition to come back to St Jude's as a staff nurse and to spend her working life at the old hospital nestling on the side of a hill by the Sussex Downs. Long before Nuala saw it, the former isolation hospital had been upgraded to a teaching hospital with new wings added, fresh departments to replace the long wards open to the sun, that had been considered essential for the many tubercular patients in years gone by.

Now that TB was a thing of the past, and many sanatoria were redundant, it was sad to see such places fall into decay. But, St Jude's was quietly establishing a reputation for surgery, and an enterprising hospital board had voted for a very prestigious private patient wing which attracted many of Britain's finest surgeons. The wing combined the best of the old building with the latest in modern equipment and was quieter than many London hospitals for the treatment of eye conditions and medical cases requiring rest.

But St Jude's wasn't the only growing concern in the area. A holiday centre about three miles away had sprung up, tending to attract a rather lively element of young people who sometimes found a need to visit the casualty department of the nearest hospital. Nuala eased the muscles of her right shoulder and winced. Last night had been bad, but possibly no worse than many such nights when a fight had been broken up by the local police and one of the boys had arrived in Casualty, threatening to fight anyone who looked at him. Nuala smiled, wryly. 'They say that we Irish are the fighters, but that lad from Liverpool beat us hollow.'

'Dreaming? Come on, Nurse Kavanagh, there's a lot to be done. You left the cubicles in a terrible mess before you swanned off for lunch.' That voice at least was one from the past and it was a voice that Nuala had hoped would no longer be at St Judes's.

'I'm sorry, Sister, but the last case had been seen and the linen hadn't come up for the afternoon.'

'I'm the best judge of that, Nurse.' Sister Frazer glanced at the clock and grunted. Nurse Kavanagh was back early and she could find no other fault with her work. 'And the last case had *not* been seen. Mr Wendover came back with a man who needed an examination and there were no clean towels in the cubicle, no fresh soap, and a ring of dirt round the wash basin.'

'There was a clean cubicle at the end, Sister. I made sure of one before I left and thought I'd hurry back from lunch to get the rest done before the afternoon session.' Nurse Kavanagh's pale face was tinged with pink and her eyes flashed with unfamiliar warmth, but she knew that she was no match for the solidly built woman who confronted her.

'Mr Wendover never uses that end cubicle. It smells of antiseptic from the minor ops theatre next door and you failed to put in a deodorant block after the abscess incision.'

'I . . . that is,' Nuala began, then her shoulders slumped. What was the good? Sister wouldn't listen if she told her that the junior had been firmly instructed to do those tasks, including making sure that the sinks at least were clean.

'I know you were off late last night when the ambulance cases came in, but that's no excuse for slackness, even if you do look as if a puff of wind would blow you away.' Sister regarded the slightly-built girl with blonde hair hanging in wisps from under the white cap with disapproval. At least she isn't the type to rush away again after a man, she thought. Who would want such a pale-faced quiet girl?

'I can't think how some girls get taken back after training, with the rank of Staff Nurse, if they haven't more control of their staff,' Sister said.

Nuala felt her eyes filling with tears. 'The Chief Nursing Officer here thought that my training at St

Jude's was sufficient recommendation for the post, Sister, even though she had never met me,' she said, with more spirit than usual. Sister Frazer pursed her lips at this sign of defiance and made it clear that in many matters she disagreed with the new and comparatively young head of nursing at St Jude's. 'Shall I do the rest of the cubicles, Sister. It is late now and the first of the afternoon patients are arriving.'

Sister nodded and walked into her office, closing the door on her parting remark about wasting time, as if it had been Nurse Kavanagh's fault that any delay had occurred. The dirty linen trolley was soon filled with crumpled towels and Nuala pushed it into the sluice room for the junior to check on the laundry list before the porter came to collect it. She went from cubicle to cubicle, checking that everything was in place and that the scrubbing bays had nail brushes and soap and bowls of freshly made-up antiseptic for rinsing hands.

Men's voices told her that students were gathering for the arrival of the surgical-firm chief. One or two of the men smiled at the new staff nurse and she recognised two who had spoken to her the day she arrived, but there was no one she knew from the old days, even though she had been away for only a year after finishing her training. The strangers added to her sense of unreality. Surely there must be someone other than Sister Frazer who was left over from the not-too-distant past?

Nuala had gone back to Ireland with hope and plans for the future. After finals, she had exchanged addresses with the rest of her set, all of whom were now scattered, one to the north, several to London hospitals, some to private clinics and one to Saudi Arabia, to a very well-paid post there.

Where were they now? At Christmas they exchanged cards, but Nuala had met only two of her old friends since that emotional parting. She looked again at the students. There had been one or two who had attracted her, but every man seemed to treat her as a young sister with whom they could laugh but have no romance. She pushed back her hair under the stupid cap that would tilt to one side. It did nothing to restrict even the tidiest hair, and she knew that her hair wasn't tidy or pretty. Just like the rest of me, she thought, ruefully.

The department now looked good, the junior nurse panted back from an errand to say that the sterilizers were full, the special gloves that Mr Wendover preferred were in the surgeon's room and the drums were in place if they were needed for dressings.

'You should be off duty, Nurse,' said Nuala. 'Why didn't you tell me?' Her slightly worried air and the soft Irish voice made the junior relax and smile. 'Go now, before Sister sees you and finds another job.' The girl tip-toed away, laughing. That's how it had been in the old days. Silly jokes that seemed funny, and harmless laughter that filled the working days. I feel more like a hundred than just twenty-two, thought Nuala.

She tapped on the office door, noticing that Sister seemed to have plenty of time to spare as she was drinking coffee with the registrar. 'Excuse me, Sister, but is there anything you'll be wanting before I report to the other clinic? I was here for the morning to fill in, but I should go over, soon.' Sister Frazer frowned. 'I do have to report to Medical Outpatients, Sister.'

'I thought you would be here all day, Nurse.' Sister Frazer turned to the registrar. 'Isn't that typical? They send me a nurse who knows my ways only to take her away again as soon as she is useful.' Sister Frazer turned and nodded curtly in dismissal, but the registrar slid from the edge of the desk where he was perched with a mug of coffee in his hand.

'Weren't you in Cas last night?' Nuala blushed red. 'That's right. It was you. Is your shoulder all right?' Sister Frazer looked from one to the other, annoyed that they seemed to know something of which she was unaware. 'Mr Wendover was looking for you, this morning. Did you see him?'

'No, I was working out in the main hall and he was in minor theatre and examining in cubicles,' said Nuala. She could find no reason to explain that she had avoided meeting the surgeon and hoped that she could escape to Medical Outpatients before they met.

'He was very concerned about you, Nurse.'

'Well, you can tell him that I'm still alive and quite well, thank you,' she said, lightly.

'Did you know what happened?' Sister had to shake her head. 'This lad came in fighting drunk and wouldn't be examined. Nurse tried to talk him round, but he was bleeding and we had to do something quickly. Blake Wendover came to examine him as no one else could get near him.' He grinned. 'Blake is quite a hunk of rugby-playing beefcake, wouldn't you say, Nurse? Should be able to handle most men, but drunks at times can be very quick and unpredictable, as Nurse learned to her cost. She tried to restrain him and he lashed out with both fists. The first blow took you by surprise and nearly knocked you off your feet, didn't it?'

She nodded, re-living the episode with horrid clarity. Instinctively, her hand went to her right shoulder. The pain had been sudden but soon over, reducing to a dull ache she barely felt as she watched the heavy boot-clad feet swing over the casualty trolley as the youth tried to stand.

'One of those bovver boots caught Blake on the side of the head just as he was bending down to help Nurse. I was worried, Sister. Blake is a powerful man, but when a blow like that takes anyone off guard, it can be dangerous.' He looked apologetic. 'We forgot about you for a time, making sure that Mr Wendover was all right.'

'I was fine. I went up to the ward with the patient. It was decided that he could calm down in a side ward before he was stitched, so the porters strapped him to the trolley and someone sat with him to make sure he stayed in a position where he couldn't inhale his vomit.' She added quickly, 'So there's no need for anyone to be worried about me.'

She went to the duty room to collect her bag and holdall so that there would be no need to come back to this department after the afternoon in Medical. So, the great man had been worried and had wanted to check that she was all right. If the registrar could be believed, Blake Wendover had come himself to ask about her. He wouldn't know my name, she thought, so he couldn't find me by

asking. Many leading surgeons would have left it to
their subordinates to track her down and enquire
politely, as a matter of courtesy but he had come
himself. Her expression softened. He might even
have seen her during the morning but not linked
her with last night's episode. How could she expect
a man like that to recall a pale face, a thin body and
a retiring manner. Even my eyes are not beautiful,
she thought, being hazel flecked with brown under
insignificant brows. She wrinkled the smooth skin
of those brows and wished that freckles would
come into fashion.

Her heart beat faster as she knew that the moment she dreaded had come. She stood back to
allow a small procession to pass her in the corridor.
It was typical of most hospitals where she had seen
students in training. First came the big boss, the
consultant. It mattered not that he was six feet tall
or five foot three, the respect for him was the same
and there was never any doubt as to his status. He
was followed by house surgeons burdened with
X-rays, notes and worried expressions, followed
closely by a gaggle of students, male and female, in
coats of varying stages of whiteness, a stethoscope
hanging self-consciously from the pocket of each
one.

Nuala held her breath and stood back as far into
the wall as she could manage. They passed in an
urgent wave of expectation, exuding power and
confidence. The man in front, who no one would
have dared to overtake in the progress to the
department, would have been impressive even
without his entourage. He was dark and tall, with
powerful shoulders and eyes that gazed darkly

under thick brows. So this was Mr Wendover in action. Nuala half hoped that he would see her and smile briefly, or pass some remark about the night before. Just to know he remembered that she tried to help him and that he smiled thanks, however impersonally, would make her aching shoulder a badge of victory. It would be useless to expect more from the man who was a world-wide authority on general surgery and lectured and demonstrated his skills in many teaching hospitals. He glanced at the pale girl by the wall, almost stopped, then went on again. Nuala had the conviction that Sister Frazer had told him who was responsible for the untidy department when he wanted to use a clean cubicle and that he now held this against her, to the exclusion of any feelings he might have about her health. Her lip trembled. She saw his glance slide away from her in the way she knew so well when men were not attracted by her. He had a fleeting impression of a pale girl whose face had been seen once, or was it that all thin nurses looked alike?

'Do I know her?' he asked, and Nuala heard the remark. The house surgeon, who had not been in Casualty the night of the fracas, shook his head.

'I doubt it, sir. She's new here.'

The surgeon glanced back and Nuala knew that something was wrong. His eyes were dark, but lack lustre, his gaze was flickering as if he couldn't focus or, if he could, then he couldn't remember what he saw. The white trail followed him and Nuala saw the swing door settle before hurrying over to Medical Outpatients. I must have been mistaken, she decided. Last night, his eyes glowed, or so I thought. They seemed to engulf me in warmth and I wanted him to touch me. The eyes she had seen in the corridor had none of that life, none of that warmth.

'Ah, there you are, Nurse Kavanagh.' Sister Odinga smiled, her eyes showing her delight in meeting an old friend. 'It's so good to see you again. Did they say I could have you here for keeps? I did ask as soon as I saw your name on the list of new arrivals. I know you are a relief nurse but I am very short-staffed.'

'Sister Odinga! You're the first friendly face I've seen since I arrived. I thought you had left to get married.'

'I did, but sanity prevailed.' She laughed. 'No, I don't mean that we broke it all off. My boyfriend needed to take another degree and we thought I might as well stay here for a while and let him take time to study while I'm working.'

'I'm happy for you, Sister.'

'You don't look it.' The searching dark eyes were gentle and warm. 'I thought you'd be married long before I got my man to the altar.'

'I thought so, too, but I'd rather not talk about it now. I can tell you later.'

'You're right.' Sister Odinga looked at the time. 'They'll be screaming for neurological trays in a minute. Be an angel and lay up a couple out there, will you, dear?'

How was it that after a full training in an absorbing and demanding career, one sister could still reduce Nuala to slow incompetence while Sister Odinga could make her feel efficient and that nothing was too much trouble to do for her? Nuala hurried to do as she was asked and anticipated every need of the man examining ears in the small dark examination room. Happiness began to bud again, small but real. If only it could be like this all the time, I could give my life to nursing and feel fulfilled, she thought. She held the tray with auroscope and swabs, the tiny jars of tincture and then took the headlamp from the consultant as he turned from his patient.

'Thank you. Nurse. I hope I have you in my clinic in future.' He smiled. 'Haven't I seen you somewhere? Some time ago?'

'I'm Nurse Kavanagh. I trained here and I've come back for a while as a relief nurse until I decide what to do.'

'Of course.' His face cleared. 'I do remember you. You worked in my ward and the patients were full of your praises.'

Her heart warmed to him. This was better. Two friendly faces with good memories of her time at St Jude's. At least two people who knew her to be good at her job. The chill of Sister Frazer's presence faded and Nuala began to forget the ugliness of the old hospital. Once more, St Jude's became the shabby friend, much loved and revered by staff and patients alike.

Dr Pierce washed his hands while the next patient was summoned. 'Now let me think,' he said. 'There have been changes here since you left.' He looked up at the ceiling as he struggled into a fresh gown. 'Old Smythe retired, you know. So did Davis. Lots of new blood, but they can't do without me yet.'

He handed her the towel that he had used when

she had given it to him as he dripped over the floor near the sink.

'I seem to have seen very few people I know,' she said.

'Have you met the new boys?'

'I met Mr Wendover yesterday and again in the corridor today,' she said. 'He didn't see me. He was on his way to his clinic.'

'First-rate chap. First-rate. How did he look to you?' She sensed his unease.

'What do you mean, sir?' She saw the reflective look in the physician's eyes. 'He went by without speaking.'

He frowned. 'He had a nasty biff on the head yesterday. An accident case came in the worse for drink and lashed out at everyone. Poor blighter had a degree of cerebral irritation from his own in-juries, but it was unfortunate that Blake Wendover should have taken the full force of his boot.' He picked up his head mirror again. 'I told him to stay away from clinics today and be quiet until he was sure he had no concussion, but you say he was doing his rounds?'

'He'd done morning rounds, a morning clinic and was on his way to the afternoon session when I saw him.'

'Well, how did he look to you?'

'I don't know what to say, sir. I don't know him at all, really. He looked tall and dark and rather pale-skinned.' Nuala looked at the man who re-garded her with such intensity. 'It's probably no-thing, Dr Pierce,' she said, and coloured. 'As I say, I hardly know him and I haven't spoken to him, but he seemed much paler this morning, and his eyes were not as bright as I thought last night.' She faltered. 'His eyes are very blue, aren't they. 'She bit her lip. That wasn't what she intended saying. 'What I mean is that his eyes seemed . . . wrong. He was tense, but I expect everyone looks fairly grim when concentrating.' She shrugged and winced at the discomfort in her shoulder.

'You were the nurse who tried to help him restrain the man last night?'

'I did more harm than good,' she replied, unhappily. 'If he hadn't bent down to help me, he would never have been kicked.'

Dr Pierce patted her hand. 'Don't worry about it. If you hadn't helped, he could have killed someone. I heard about it.' She moved restlessly. 'And you have a feeling that something is wrong, just as I have,' he said, quietly. 'Is he in the clinic now?'

'I think so. Shall I get Sister to bleep him or ring the department?'

'No, leave it. Nothing more distracting than those stupid bells buzzing all over the place. Progress! If I want a message sent, I'd rather send a pretty nurse with it. Much less trying to the nerves. I will not have some contraption startling the life out of me in my pocket.'

'So that's why we can't get hold of you when we need you,' said Sister Odinga, looking in to see what was delaying the physician. She tried to sound cross, but, as usual, her wide smile and dancing eyes gave the lie to her words. 'Did I hear the name Mr Wendover? I held up the flow of patients as he is in my office waiting to see you.' She looked from one serious face to the other. 'You think there's something wrong, too?' Nuala was startled. 'Nurse

Kavanagh made me uneasy about him when she mentioned him so I took a close look just now. I don't know why he's here now, but I think you should see him soon, Dr Pierce.' She turned to Nuala. 'Please bring an ophthalmoscope, an auroscope, a headlamp and reflector, Nurse.'

Nurse Kavanagh ran to the clinical room and swiftly gathered the implements. She hurried back and heard voices in the dark examination room. 'I'm going to go through the whole examination, Blake. No, it's no use looking like a cross little boy. Keep that for the band of adoring females who pant after you. Thank you, Nurse.' He turned to take the tray, and the light from his headlamp dazzled her. She turned her head to avoid the glare, then the light was gone and she was used to the gloom once more. Blake Wendover stood by the chair, defensively. For the second time that day he glanced at the little nurse with the pale face and freckled nose. He put a hand over his eyes.

'Take a message to Theatre,' said Sister Odinga in a whisper. 'Dr Pierce insists that Mr Wendover is in no fit state to take the case admitted. Tell Theatre Sister that the registrar must cope or get the next emergency surgeon on the list. Come back here before you go off duty if you don't mind, as I need someone to answer the phone and my other nurses have gone to tea.'

'I'll get back quickly and stay for as long as you want me,' said Nurse Kavanagh.

'Bless you. It's good to have someone I can trust and who is sensible.'

Nuala went away with feelings of anxiety and pride. The hospital was once more involving her in its drama and its day-to-day work. The theatre was as she recalled, but it now had the addition of a heart-lung apparatus and the anaesthetic room was refitted. Not my favourite place, she decided, and gave her message to a surprised and very concerned theatre sister. Everyone thought well of the surgeon with the dark blue eyes and Nuala wished that those eyes had registered more than puzzlement the last time they saw her. The porter paused to listen to what was said. He lifted the drums on to the racks and lost his cheery smile, and the junior nurse blushed as if personally involved. Nuala knew instinctively that the nurse was one of the many who carried a torch for the handsome surgeon.

We all did that, during training, she remembered. It seemed so long ago, when she had felt like that for a man who was a god in her eyes until he lost his temper in the theatre one day and threw a dirty swab at her. She smiled, slightly. It was the end of the world for quite half a day, each time he shouted out the deficiencies of the theatre staff he made the students grin with relief if they, for once, were not the cause of his wrath.

She was back at the door of the examination room and tapped gently. 'Sister Odinga?'

The slim, dark sister came to the door and closed it behind her. 'All set? He's having a tussle with Dr Pierce in there. I don't want him to know what is happening behind his back, so I'd like you to keep out of there. He knew that we sent a message about him but he is convinced that he is well enough to operate. You should be off duty.'

'It isn't important. I'll stay by the phone until you

finish the clinic and avoid Mr Wendover if he comes out with Dr Pierce.' She hesitated. 'He didn't seem to recognise me, Sister. There's no reason why he should remember me from last night, but he did see me face to face in the corridor and looked puzzled as if struggling to remember.'

Sister Odinga looked solemn. 'I'll tell Dr Pierce. He has been trying to find out if there was a period of amnesia between the blow and recovery and it might be so. He recalls most of what happened, but he's obviously suffering from delayed shock and a degree of concussion.' She saw the girl's stricken face. 'Cheer up. He may be quite all right. He thinks he's indispensable, as do we all, and we must protect him from his over-developed urge to do his duty.'

'But Dr Pierce thinks there is something badly wrong, doesn't he?'

'He wants to ward him for further observation. There is a possibility of damage to one eye.'

'But the eyes were not hurt.'

'You know as well as I do that it isn't necessary for someone to have black eyes before they have eye injuries. A sharp blow can injure the optic nerve from the brain to the eye. It could mean that the retina at the back of the eye is inflamed.'

'Could it be detached?' Nuala was cold.

'I hope to goodness it is not. It may be only a simple inflammation. Heaven knows what would happen if that lovely man couldn't . . . oh, the possibility is unthinkable.' Sister Odinga's face was sad as she turned away. 'He's a wonderful person, Kavanagh. I wish you could get to know him. He's a wonderful man.'

Somewhere behind that blank cold look there had to be warmth. Nuala had glimpsed it before he had chilled her with his uncomprehending glance in the corridor. Every person who mentioned him made similar remarks about his skill, his humour, his attraction for women. Trusted colleagues like the theatre sister and the sister in Outpatients held him in high regard, and even Sister Frazer could speak of him without the curl of the lip that said that the new men were not a patch on the old school of surgeons that she knew. Pretty nurses hung on his words and dropped instruments in their efforts to impress him and the students liked his direct manner and fair dealing.

She wondered if there had been sparks of admiration in those dark eyes for any of the very pretty nurses on the staff of St Jude's. The little nurse in the theatre fluttered her eyelashes at anyone in trousers and would probably marry a doctor. She sighed. How many times had men appeared to be friendly, only to let their attention wander the moment a pretty girl with more bosom than sense came into his sights? For the first time since leaving Ireland, she forced herself to think of Dermot, the good-looking man with the sensual mouth who had been her friend since school days. Both families had taken it for granted that they would marry in time, walking up the aisle of the local church that they had known since they were infants, and Dermot had played along with this reasoning. It was pleasant to have a good-looking boy as a companion, but as they grew up, she had lost her puppy charm and colour, growing pale and more freckled as each summer passed, while Dermot grew into a handsome man with bright blue eyes and fair skin, a slight, tall body and the hands of an artist.

She shivered as she recalled those hands when he tried to make love to her. She had pulled away from his kisses, laughing and trying to pass it off as a joke, thrusting away the growing belief that he had no respect for her and wanted only to seduce her with no thought of marriage. He had sulked all the way home from the wild hillside where he had kissed her so differently from his earlier kisses. She had looked at the sullen face and watched the beautiful hands tearing the grass head to pieces on the way back to the village and the sharp look her mother gave her was accusing and devoid of sympathy.

Somehow, the rumour had spread over the village that Nuala Kavanagh had lost her virginity and it was only after her brother fought Dermot and made him retract the lie that the mud settled. I couldn't stay there after that, she thought. He told me quite plainly that if I wouldn't go with him, there were plenty who would and they had more to offer. The memory was not quite as bad now that St Jude's had taken her into its refuge, but it still rankled.

'Oh, come on,' she whispered. It was bad enough to have nothing to do but wait by the telephone to intercept calls and so not disturb either Sister Odinga or Dr Pierce while Mr Wendover was being examined, but to let her mind go back to the unhappy time in Ireland added a greater burden. She stared at the closed door, wondering what was happening on the other side, but it made her feel even worse. The memory of those dark eyes haunted her as no eyes of any patient had done during her association with the profession.

CHAPTER TWO

THE second time the telephone rang, Nurse Kavanagh answered it while looking at the closed door of the examination room. They would be coming out soon and the last person she wanted to see was Mr Wendover, angry because he had been delayed by a fussy physician who insisted on carrying out every conceivable test for eye and brain damage and refused to let him go to the theatre to get on with his urgent case.

The message was brief and Nuala put down the telephone and went quickly to the sluice room to find the nurse who had come back on duty. I suppose I could go off duty now they are back from tea, she thought, but knew that this was impossible. She longed to open that door and to know what was happening. She hated the limbo of silence that added to her dread and concern. Her eyes felt hot and prickly and she tried to remember that the registrar had insisted that she had helped Mr Wendover and she was in no way responsible for his injury, but she had a growing conviction that if he had not bent down to help her after the man struck her, he would not be sitting in an examination chair facing bright lights and X-rays.

The door opened and Nuala fled to the sluice room. Sister Odinga came after her and seemed relieved to know that she was still waiting.

'How is he, Sister?' Nuala asked.

Sister Odinga scribbled on a memo pad and tore off the top sheet of paper. 'Would you take this to the private wing and give it to Sister. If she isn't there, find out where she is as I know she is on duty. Give the message to her alone. I can't ring the wing as he might hear me talking and I can't leave here just now. She will ask you questions about him. Tell her all you know, but make sure you are alone when you do so as he would be very upset if the whole hospital gossiped about his condition before we know for certain what is wrong.'

Nuala wasted no time in fruitless questions. The lift took her up to the private block and, in a minute, she was walking along the more luxurious corridor leading to the wing. It was modern inside the old shell of an office and administration department, using the space to the best effect and yet losing none of the charm of old wood where it had been possible to retain it. The patients nursed in the wing paid over the odds for treatment and the privilege of being admitted at their own convenience. If the case was an emergency there was little advantage in paying huge fees unless privacy rated high, or the telephone link with the outside world that made each room a tiny home and office was required. The fitted furniture was well-designed and the crisp curtains and covers carried a colour theme through the fitted carpets and flower prints on the walls.

A huge bowl of daffodils graced the walnut table by Sister's office and fine hunting prints hung in the foyer. It's like a luxury hotel, thought Nuala, who could remember being within the hallowed walls only once during her training. Sister asked her into

the office as soon as she understood that the message was private. Here again, there were subtle
touches of extra comfort. Amber curtains were
caught back from the windows with wide swathes of
gold brocade and the chairs were upholstered in a
toning fabric. When important patients were
admitted, their relatives and friends could find
similar comforts and reassurance in such surroundings and it was probably responsible for calming
many fears to be met with such restful elegance.

Sister scanned the note and frowned. 'Did you
see him, Nurse?'

Nuala cast an anxious glance behind her and saw
that the door was closed. 'Yes, I saw him before Dr
Pierce took over. There was something very
strange about his eyes and I think he was suffering
from delayed shock and concussion when I saw
him. Sister Odinga says that a diagnosis hasn't yet
been reached, but they fear he might have a detached retina or at least a badly inflamed one. I
thought he was trying to hide the fact that he was in
pain, but, of course, I don't know him and it might
just have been anger at being delayed.'

'I wouldn't think he was angry. If Dr Pierce
thinks he needs treatment, Blake Wendover would
accept his decision. He would never be petty about
anything.' She read the note again. 'Tell me about
it. How did it happen?'

Nuala told her of the man in Casualty, but glos-
sed over her own part in it. 'Dr Pierce seemed very
concerned,' she added.

'I would imagine that everyone who met Blake
Wendover would feel the same, Nurse. You like
him, don't you?'

'I don't know him. I haven't really met him; at least, not to speak to him. He wasn't here before I went back to Ireland after I finished training last year.'

'I knew I'd seen you somewhere. Didn't you special those babies on Ward Six?'

Nuala blushed. 'I can't think how you can remember that, Sister. It was over two years ago.'

'I heard great things about you and I even asked if you could come here if you applied for a job after training.' Nuala looked surprised. 'Did no one tell you?'

'They said nothing about the wing. The matron, that is, Miss Steed, who was here before the present Senior Nursing Officer, said that there was work for me if I wanted it, but I was planning to go home to Ireland.'

'And now you are doing relief work?' Sister French looked thoughtful. 'I prefer to have Jude's nursing on my wing and we never get enough trained staff applying to come back. Would you enjoy working with me for a while, if I could arrange it? Would you come on the staff as permanent private patient personnel?'

Nuala smiled. The contrast between the formidable Sister Frazer and this pleasant young sister was too much. 'After Casualty and Outpatients, this would be heaven, Sister.' She glanced round the office. 'It would be warm here. The chill wind that blows through the empty clinics is a shock in itself. I should have remembered that, but it took me by surprise. Half the nurses working there are off with colds. That's why I was needed.'

'Are you on duty tomorrow?'

'No, Sister. I have a day off and an early morning after that. I report to Admin. at two and I have no idea where they want me to go then.'

'I'll speak to Miss Bell, but I'd like to have some idea of how long you intend staying at St Jude's.'

'I can't really say at the moment, Sister. I have no immediate plans and I wanted to be a relief nurse to give me some flexibility, but I would like to work here.'

'Thank Sister for the note and tell her I shall do as she suggests. I hope to see you soon, Nurse. It would be good to have someone who could stay for a long time and be happy here.' Sister French smiled brightly, hoping to spark off a similar reaction in the pale girl with hazel eyes. A pity she has quite so many freckles, she thought. Such dainty hands and feet, but something holding her back from showing any positive emotion. 'Are you worried about him,' she asked, suddenly aware that guilt could have the same effect on a girl who thought she might be responsible for the accident.

'I think we are all worried,' said Nuala, quietly. Sister sighed. It was plain that Nurse Kavanagh was not ready to take her into her confidence. Just as well we have some plain Janes to dedicate themselves to a lifetime of work and devotion, she decided.

On her way from the wing, Nuala passed the beautiful table again, now covered with a fresh delivery of flowers. She peeped at one card stuck into a bouquet of orchids and saw that they were intended for a very famous film star. Nothing had been said about her being a patient at St Jude's and

Nuala recalled reading an article about her and the holiday she was enjoying in South Africa. She smiled. Such privacy within travelling distance of London was worth a lot to people needing rest and complete anonymity. To live a life in a goldfish bowl of publicity must be a terrific strain and the calm of the wing could be therapeutic even before medical treatment was started. It would be fascinating to work in the wing.

Sister Odinga was waiting for her. She was carrying a cloak, ready to go off duty. 'We're both very late, Kavanagh,' she said. 'Mr Wendover is in good hands and seems resigned to being admitted to the wing. Did you see him on his way up?'

'No, I came by the stairs, but I heard something in the lift. Can you tell me what happened?'

'He went quietly, but it was very difficult for him. The stronger and more intelligent a man is, the worse he can be when he has to hand over control to lesser mortals. He hates being restricted and I expect that Sister French will have to be firm with him. He seemed quiet enough, but of course, he's still in secondary shock.' She saw the stricken look on the girl's face. 'Come on, Kavanagh, cheer up. You did your best and nearly had the same injury yourself. There's no need to take the accident so personally. Come and have supper with me. I want to hear about that boyfriend of yours.'

Nuala shook her head. 'I can't.'

'Come on, now. You have to talk to someone. I recall a time when I cried on your shoulder,' she said, softly. 'It was such a relief to talk to someone and I didn't care that I lost dignity in the process.'

'That you never did,' said Nuala.

'Well, then, I'm here to help you if help you need. I never liked protocol and off duty we were friends.'

'I'd like to have supper with you,' said Nuala. She managed a smile and felt more warm and wanted than she had done since coming back to St Jude's. She was surprised that Odinga recalled the occasion when the more senior nurse had broken down and wept on receiving the news that her mother was dead. It happened far away in Africa, where her daughter could not see her and couldn't even attend the funeral. Nuala had held her close, murmuring as she would to a child, while the night passed and the girl's anguish ran dry. We have wakes in Ireland for death, thought Nuala, but no wakes for broken hearts and wounded pride.

The cafeteria was comfortable and the supper provided for a subsidised price was good. The two girls lingered over their food and talked about general things as others sat at their table. No mention could be made of the surgeon who was now resting in the private patients' wing without more than a handful of people knowing about it. 'Come back to my room for coffee,' said Nuala. They walked to the accommodation block, next to the hospital, but not a part of it. Nuala was pleased with the pretty room she had there and found it very convenient to be so near to her work.

'I have a flat further along the road which is almost as near, but this must be good if you are late for duty,' said Odinga. The small kitchen at the end of a corridor was basic and functional and served six rooms on the same landing, rather like being in a university hall of residence. They took coffee back to Nuala's room rather than risk being overheard in the communal sitting-room downstairs.

'Blake Wendover does seem to have a slight degree of amnesia,' said Odinga when they were in the room, drinking coffee. 'I was very glad to see him put into a wheel chair and taken to the wing. Dr Pierce was waiting for the wet plates from the portable X-ray to come back before deciding on the best treatment.'

'Do they suspect a fracture as well?'

'Nothing can be ruled out at this stage. A piece of bone splinter could cause the pressure and of course that would mean surgery. If there is only bruising or a damaged nerve, then rest and possibly laser therapy if the retina is detached will be routine.'

'And his sight?'

Odinga sipped her coffee, her huge dark eyes eloquent. 'I hate to even consider it.' She yawned. 'Some people have time off tomorrow, but I have to be on duty early. And you haven't even told me about Dermot.'

'No, I nearly forgot about him,' said Nuala with an air of surprise.

'I noticed,' said Odinga, dryly. 'I think you have finished with that affair, Kav.'

'It wasn't even that,' said Nuala. 'He wanted that but I couldn't,' she said, simply.

'Very wise if you aren't in love.' Odinga struggled up from the foam plastic chair and shrugged into her cloak. 'I hate English winters,' she said. 'The end of February seems even colder than January every year. I tell myself that tomorrow the sun will shine, and hope for warmth.' Nuala saw her to the main door and watched her walking up the road towards her own apartment. Even under the bad street lighting, she was graceful and attractive. If I was more like that, I would be happy, thought the girl who had long ago decided that she had no redeeming features at all, forgetting that her feet were enviably small, her hands well-shaped and delicate, and her skin, though pale and freckled, was free of blemishes.

Wearily, she bathed and then sat for a while, reading. Wrapped in the thick dressing gown and velvet mules that had formed a part of her bottom drawer and been intended to be worn when she married Dermot, she was cosy. It had been a busy day, full of excitement. She didn't envy Dr Pierce if he had to tell Mr Wendover what to do, she thought. Everyone told her that the great man was wonderful and he seemed almost too good to be true, but she knew that he could be impatient at times from snippets heard in Casualty, and that firm jaw wasn't the sign of a meek and accepting personality. She told herself that Dr Pierce would give the best care possible, the best chance of recovery, and everything possible would be done for the full and safe recovery of his health and sight, but she found herself thinking the same phrases, again and again. Full recovery of health and sight. Best treatment possible. I'm trying to convince myself, she thought, and wondered if Mr Wendover was still awake in his pretty room.

Before she turned out her light, she slipped her dressing gown from her right shoulder and saw that a dark bruise had formed. It ached more now after a day of work and she massaged it as best she could with adrenalin cream which took away the soreness and allowed her to sleep. In her dream, she was offering soothing creams to a man with eyes bandaged, but he didn't know she was there. She turned sharply and lay on the bruised shoulder, moaning slightly as she felt the ache again. She got up and put on more cream and went back to sleep for uneasy rest until morning came and the footsteps of nurses hurrying down to breakfast stirred her to full wakefulness. The heaviness of a bad night remained with her as she took a really hot shower and let the sharp water pepper her shoulder with heat. It was better and she applied more cream, moving her muscles more easily and smiling her relief.

Her dreams haunted her still as she went across to late breakfast in the main dining room. She tried to think of home and of what she wanted to do on this day off, but she thought of the man with bandaged eyes, and shuddered as she recalled a painting of a man in darkness with powerful shoulders and an air of defeat. She could see again the blind Samson, completely lost. It can't happen to him. It must never happen to Blake Wendover.

Two letters waited for her at the lodge and she took them with her to breakfast. She hurried to the dining room used for breakfast and for the meal for night nurses coming off duty. The room was lofty, cannibalised from the old refectory but now boasting modern chairs and tables and an efficient hot plate for nurses' breakfasts on days off. These could be reserved by signing a book overnight and was used for those taking exams as well as for off duty arrangements. At least I've finished with exams, Nuala thought, with relief. They had never been her strong point and it was a dread of exams that had prevented her from going with some of her set to take a midwifery course. Or was she deceiving herself? It would be more true to admit that she had wanted to finish her general training and go home to marry Dermot, have children and settle down in the part of Ireland that was dear to her.

I must plan my life, she thought. She felt a flutter of real panic when she saw the handwriting on the envelope of the letter. Her mother's handwriting made Nuala tear open that envelope first. As usual, the letter was brief. A husband and five children had left Mrs Kavanagh with little time and no desire for writing letters and even now, when her children were grown and all away from home except for Michael, the youngest son and as yet unmarried, to his mother's private satisfaction as he had been her favourite since his birth, she wrote little. Most of the news was about Michael and no mention was made of the other children. Dermot had been asking about her, Nuala read.

She held the letter tightly, crumpling the edges in her annoyance. The nerve of him to ask after her when he knew that she wished never to see him again! But Mrs Kavanagh didn't seem a bit put out by the visit and made no mention of his attempt to humiliate her daughter. 'He wants to see you again, Nuala. Surely you can overlook what he did. He assures me that it was all a joke and he would do you no harm. A silly boyish bit of nonsense happens between all young people and I'm inclined to believe him.'

Nuala could hardly read on. Her mother had a soft spot for the good-looking boy and he had only to praise her cooking and give her a hug to make her blush with pleasure. She nearly choked on a crust of toast as she followed the words. He could charm the birds out of the trees if he gave his mind to it, as Nuala knew to her cost, but her mother should know better, having watched him grow up. She went over the last words again. It couldn't be true. He wanted to come to England to see her. He was talking of seeing her with a view to patching up the silly quarrel and fixing an early date for the wedding.

'You will see him? I've told him that I know you are still fond of him.' Nuala thrust the letter into her bag and went back to eating breakfast. The eggs and bacon were fast congealing on the plate and she drank some coffee to try to wash down the unappetising food, but found that she could swallow nothing. Her mother had not said when Dermot might come to England and she had no idea where he would stay in the district if he came to see her. London was quite accessible by train and bus or taxi from the small station in the next village, or rather the small town it had become since the growth of the hospital and the holiday centre over the hills. There was only one good hotel for miles and one small pub.

She was too unsettled to stay in and read or to press the clothes she had washed two days ago, and the second letter with its typewritten address could only be official and boring if not actually disturbing, and she had no mental energy left to read it.

In the old days, there would have been someone

in her own set to go with her on a day off, even if
there was nothing special for them to do. Some of
her most enjoyable days of leisure had been spent
just walking, looking in shop windows or buying
something wildly extravagant like new lipstick!
There would be a bus to the town in ten minutes
and she decided to catch it rather than sit in her
room and mope about times past. The sky held grey
clouds and the wind was cold. Nuala ran back to her
room for an umbrella, but wondered if it would be
usable in such gusty conditions. A head scarf would
be better and would at least keep her hair in some
sort of order. She dashed to the bus stop and
managed to get a window seat just before the bus
started off.

She had hoped that putting some distance between herself and the hospital would help her to
forget the events of the past two days, but each tree
that flashed its bare branches as the bus gathered
speed seemed to have the hint of a man's head in
the shape. I must make up my mind about two
things, she told herself firmly. I mustn't think of
work and in particular I must put Mr Wendover out
of my mind for the day. I can't enquire about him
and I have no right to visit the wing during my
off-duty unless I'm invited. The other matter is
more long-term and complicated. I have to leave
the past behind me. I have to take on a fresh image
and to be so different that even my family will know
that I am serious about wanting to plan my own
future without Dermot.

She gazed out of the smudged window and
caught sight of her own reflection. I look like an
Orphan Annie, she thought, impatiently. A thin

girl in a drab-coloured head scarf with no make-up except lipstick of a colour that goes with nothing in particular. I ought to have done something about my appearance long ago instead of allowing the family to crush any ideas I might have of improving my looks. Her mother had dismissed make-up as mere vanity and as for wasting good money on expensive hair styling, well that was sinful. A dominant family had soon laughed away her efforts in those directions as soon as she returned to them after training. Her mother hinted that the money would be better spent on Michael as he was earning nothing.

They don't really care. They laugh at me and hope I will do as they want, but what of my feelings? For the first time in her life, she thought, she hated her family, and the fact that her mother could condone Dermot's actions came as a shock that would take a long time to heal, so it was with an air of defiance that she stepped off the bus and looked for a coffee shop. There was a good place, she remembered at the end of the old part of the village, overlooking wide fields with a good view of the Downs. She poured coffee and stared out over the drenched fields. Some signs of spring appeared in the loose tilth of ploughed fields and a faint haze of green showed in the hedgerows. At home, the sea would be sparkling in rare bursts of sunshine. She tried to forget the beach she loved. I may never go back again, she thought, sadly. They can't love me if they want me to marry a man who showed no respect for me and went with other women.

The coffee was good and she drank more, nibbling crisp chocolate biscuits that were her favourites. Her anger was soon mixed with unwilling humour. They want me married in case I end up an old maid, so it doesn't matter who the man might be. If I said I wanted to be a nun, they'd be delighted, but failing that, any man, even one who tried to seduce me, will gain respectability. Well, I shall stay here, have my hair cut and buy a new dress, she decided.

The idea pleased her. After all, she had some money, the time to spare and the need to take her mind from the hospital, so why not spoil herself for once? She looked in all the shops and found that two new boutiques had appeared since her time at St Jude's. One was full of rather bright and way-out clothes, but the other window was filled with an optimistic display of spring clothes. The flowers in the tall white vases were fake but the general result was good and it made a cheerful change to look at pretty garments.

Nuala pushed dresses along the rail and had second thoughts about buying. I have enough clothes, she thought and who is there to bother how I look? The last person she wanted to impress was Dermot, the only man who showed any desire to see her. But it was in defiance that she held up a floral dress in front of her and looked over it at the long mirror. A girl came to help her, smiling. 'Aren't you lucky to be so slim,' she said.

'Thin,' Nuala corrected her.

'Not with those feet and hands. Just slim and in proportion.' She frowned. 'But that is too busy for you. You need something good to make you stand out in a crowd, but not that. It swamps you.'

'I don't think I'll bother,' said Nuala.

'This rail is all your size. We have reduced them because there aren't many people small enough to wear them, but they are wonderful value.' She selected a dress of fine wool with a swirling skirt. 'Try it on.'

'I've never worn violet in my life,' protested Nuala. She handled the dress and knew that it was a great bargain. The full sleeves tapered into tightly fitting cuffs that were buttoned with tiny gold catches and the bodice looked well cut. 'All right, but I think that plain dark green is more me.' She went into the fitting room and slipped the deep violet dress over her head. Her hair seemed even more spiky than usual and she combed it back. The bodice fitted perfectly and followed the gentle curves of her bosom in a way that she found strange and unexpected. The girl sighed with pleasure when Nuala went out to see what her reaction would be.

'But I can't wear it,' said the unwilling model.

'If I could get into that one, it would have been sold the day I saw it,' said the assistant. 'It's perfect for most occasions and very flattering. With your pale skin it glows and when you've been for your hair appointment, and put on the right make-up, you'll be delighted.'

'Hair appointment?'

'This weather is terrible. I see that you have hair rather like mine. I keep it short like this to make it behave and I think it suits me.' Nuala stared at the pretty hair style that was so different from her own straggly locks. 'Have you tried Henri up near the old market place? I go to him and have a cleanse and make-up when I have a decent commission,' said the girl. 'You will have this?' She took the dress from the hand that held it through the opening in the cubicle curtains and began to pack it.

'I didn't say,' began Nuala, but the sales girl had gone safely out of sight and hearing. 'Ah, well, live dangerously, for once.' She pulled her hair up through a band and knotted it on top of her head before putting the scarf back over it. As soon as she was dressed, she went to pay for the dress and looked at the girl serving her. 'Is Henri very busy or do I have to make an appointment?' asked Nuala, slowly. If I have that dress, I shall have to get my hair cut or something, she decided.

'Have some lunch, but make an appointment for early afternoon. There's usually a lull then before people come in for shopping. Tell him you want it like Mary-at-the-shop and he'll do it himself, if you like this style.'

With rising excitement, Nuala went to the salon and, almost to her horror, they could fit in an appointment at two. The scented pink and pale mauve curtains and the piped muzak lulled her into a sensual dreamlike state as she sat and resigned herself to her fate. Henri raised an eyebrow when he first combed out her hair, but made no sarcastic comments as he snipped and shaped. The hair was washed and set and Nuala was popped under a hot dryer like a loaf into an oven, she thought, turning down the heat slightly and picking up a glossy magazine to read while she cooked.

The recklessness caused by her resolve to be different made her nod when a cleanse and make-up was suggested and she stared at the result of the afternoon's work as if she was seeing a stranger. The freckles had been toned down to an acceptable haze under warm foundation and her eyes seemed to glow under faint brown shadows that made the flecks in the hazel depths more pronounced. Henri left her to the mercy of a good salesgirl who sold her the complete range of make-up and made sure she knew what to use for day and evening wear. In vain, Nuala protested that she never went anywhere worth the trouble, and felt humbled when the girl said that it didn't matter. Women dressed to please themselves, didn't they? Men were not as important as they liked to believe. This was accompanied by a sniff that hinted that men were a constant source of irritation to the good-looking girl.

Numbed with attention, Nuala took out the letter with the typed envelope and saw with surprise that it was from Dermot. He said that he had addressed the letter in that way in case she saw his handwriting and threw it away unread. She smiled, wondering what could have made him write. She knew that little-boy-hurt manner and it came across on paper as well as if he was in front of her. She skipped over the protestations of sorrow and his plea for forgiveness without emotion. A few months ago, this letter would have sent her in a flurry of eagerness to the nearest telephone or at least to find writing paper and stamps. It was the letter of a man in love who wanted to marry her. Its urgency was, dare she say it, puzzling? If she was the unattractive girl he had said she was at their last meeting, surely there was no rush to get her to the altar? Some of his words touched a part of her mind deeply, but an annoying doubt kept coming to the surface. She tried not to think that it breathed of insincerity.

All the way back to the hospital, she was pensive but calm. At least I can hold up my head again with this letter in my bag, proving that he did ask me to marry him, she thought, but the knowledge gave her no real joy and none of the satisfaction it would have given her at one time. She saw two faces now, the good-looking but weak mouth of the Irishman and the tawny-dark hair and firm chin of a man in pain, and it was impossible not to compare the two.

St Jude's was a haven from the cold and from her thoughts. In the cafeteria she was greeted by one of her old set and she sat with her to hear her news and to drink tea before she rushed back on duty.

'I am Junior Theatre Sister in "A" theatre,' said Maggie Rich. 'I didn't know you were here.' She seemed pleased to see her old friend and they arranged to meet when they could be off duty together. 'Must dash now. I only came down for a quick break. We had a panic on this morning.' Nuala tried not to think about theatres. 'You know they made theatre "A" into eyes and orthopaedics, one in each section?'

'No, I didn't know,' said Nuala, quickly. 'What was the panic?' It would be terrible to wish an accident on any other person and to hope that the case was for bone surgery, but she prayed that it wasn't Mr Wendover who had gone to theatre.

Maggie gulped more tea and looked at her watch again. 'They haven't sent for me so I suppose they can cope for five more minutes. The case? Oh, it didn't come off after all. A bit mysterious, but some of PP do seem to be like that if the patient is a VIF who wants no news boys pestering him for interviews before he is out of anaesthetic and back to bed,' she said, cheerfully.

'You don't know who it was?' Nuala tried to hold the cup steadily, but put it down on the saucer.

'An eye case, but they decided he wasn't ready. No name, but it was rumoured that he might be a member of staff. I didn't see him and he might be a student or a member of admin; they like their privacy.'

'Probably.'

'The theatre superintendent made me stay on call, but she didn't have me back on duty. She said I might be needed and would I stay in the hospital or in my room. A bit steep if I want to go into town, but he must be important.'

'They might still take him to theatre?'

'An injured retina, I heard. Mr Micheljon looked in at him and decided to leave it alone until some minor contusions have settled. He likes his patients on a simple regime and an umbrella dose of antibiotics to combat infection before he does anything very heroic.'

'So you think he might go home to wait for developments?'

'I've no idea. Someone said he was on the staff here and that often means a long way to get home. I would think that unless he lives locally with his family, Mr Micheljon would want him under observation. Travelling wouldn't do him much good, would it?'

Nuala shook her head, silently hoping that the patient might be some other, anonymous man who had less to lose, less to give the world than Mr

Wendover, but she knew that it was highly likely that he was the patient who had kept the theatre staff alerted for action. He couldn't be spared from the good work he did, she argued. A man with so much expertise, so much humanity must be allowed to give all he had of value. The junior theatre sister left in a hurry and Nuala went to her room, deep in thought.

The letter from Dermot had been almost forgotten in her concern for the man in the private wing and she put it in a drawer without reading it again. If he comes to see me, I can't stop him, she thought, but I don't think it will change anything. She could think of him without anger now, and her pride was soothed by the knowledge that he now wanted to marry her. It was a rounding off of her affairs, the transition from one kind of life to another. There is so much to do here in this hospital if I never marry, she thought. I could stay here and build up a wonderful career . . .

Sister Odinga looked in to chat on her way to bed and to give Nuala a message. 'Oh, I'm glad I found you. Admin. weren't sure if you were sleeping in the home or visiting friends. You are off tomorrow morning after your day off, aren't you?'

'I should be off until two.'

'Could you report to Admin. before lunch to get your instructions? It just means being in the hospital a little early and not having a lunch date if that's what you had planned.'

'I had no plans,' said Nuala. 'Have you any idea where I'm to go? I hoped I might do a stint with you.'

'No such luck, I'm afraid. I did ask, but the whole

place is screaming for extra staff and I am not too badly off now that Nurse Brown has come back from leave.'

Nuala offered her coffee and they sat talking until midnight. Odinga was interested in the story of Dermot and viewed his sudden change of mind with great suspicion.

'Perhaps he does miss me more than he realised,' said Nuala.

'I think he is one big slippery fish,' said Odinga. 'I think there is more about him that you will hear. I can't think how your mother can encourage him if she cares for you.'

'She wants to see me married. I can understand her in a way. Mothers of big families can never give their full attention to each child and one settled and giving no further cause for concern is a great help, but it does make me think that I would be better off staying away from home for a while until I have decided what to do.'

'Is that why you made the great decision, today?'

'What decision?'

'Your hair. Really, Kav, you look very good. I like it very much and you'll have no difficulty with it on duty.'

'I'd almost forgotten.' Nuala smiled. 'I went mad and bought a dress, too. I was talked into it but I think it might be useful if there are any hospital jollys to go to.'

It was only when Odinga stood up and stretched, ready to leave, that Nuala licked her dry lips and dared to ask if she had any news of Blake Wendover.

'He's being awkward, I think, from the little that

French told me. We still try to keep his presence quiet and to do that, they brought in a nurse from an agency who knows nothing about the people here, and he detests her voice.'

'Is that important? If she's good at her work, she can't upset him, surely, and if he's just waiting for treatment she can't have much to do.'

Odinga glanced at her, sharply. 'Didn't you know? Both his eyes are bandaged to ensure that they rest. He is on complete bed rest for the time being, so all the other senses are important: touch and smell and noise. Sounds are heard more acutely and voices are very important.'

CHAPTER THREE

'Come in,' The voice was crisp. 'Ah, Nurse Kavanagh, I want you to work on the private patient
wing for a while. Sister French suggested you and as
you are a relief nurse with no firm ties to any
department, I see no reason for you to go back to
Outpatients where Sister Frazer now has her full
complement of staff returning after sick leave.' She
looked up. 'What is it, Nurse? You don't look too
happy about it.' The senior nursing officer allowed herself a slight smile. 'Don't tell me you'd
rather work in that draughty old place with Sister
Frazer?'

'No, Sister.' Her voice was soft. 'I'd like to work
with Sister French. Do you know if I'll be on
general duties?'

'That's for Sister French to decide, but she did
stress that she would want you there for some time
to come as she wants a certain continuity, as she put
it.'

Nuala walked to the lift, pressed the button and
ascended to the private wing. The atmosphere of
calm and luxury was as it had been the first time she
saw it, but her own reactions were quite different.
She passed the table piled high once more with
beautiful blooms in bunches, in strait-laced tor-
tured bouquets and in pots. The cards were often
scented and some of the orchids must surely have
been flown from the most exotic regions of the

world, while the heady perfume from a dense mass of Riviera carnations had an Italian message.

One name took her attention and she paused to read the card. 'For my darling Blake with all my love, Trudie.'

Sister French was warmly welcoming. 'I wondered if she'd let you come, but now you have, I shan't let you go in a hurry. I hope you'll consider coming on the staff here as a permanent arrangement. I want you to special Mr Wendover. He was warded soon after you left and they have decided to give him complete rest in darkness as the preliminary treatment before they decide what to do for the long term.'

'What do you want me to do?'

'Mr Micheljon will come each morning to instil Atropine drops. This will be done in the darkened room so that no light reaches that eye. Both eyes will rest completely although they think that the right one might be all right. It's too early to be sure, and if they let him use that eye, it could affect both eyes adversely. One might get worse in smypathy; it does happen. You come on at eight in the morning, lay up the tray for Mr Micheljon and then stand by the door and allow no one to go in. That includes me, other doctors, the Queen or the Pope! Nobody enters until Mr Micheljon comes out again.' Nuala nodded. 'You will do all the usual things. You coax or bully him into having blanket baths, drinking moderate amounts of water or soft drinks and make him eat well. You keep him comfortable and as happy as can be expected of someone already acting as if he's in a cage.'

'Is he being difficult, Sister?'

'A little, but that will be up to you to make sure he keeps happy. During the afternoon, another nurse will relieve you and you can take an extra hour off duty as I shall need you to settle him last thing at night. I'm sorry about this, but he hates change and we want him to have no cause for complaint. As yet, that has been his only grumble, that the staff changes and he has to get used to many voices, many personalities. He can't get to know any one person, and I think a quiet little thing like you might be good for him.'

'I'll do my best, Sister.' The whole business had an unreal sense of inevitability. In her dream, she had seen him against white pillows, and as she entered his room, softly, but making enough noise to let him know he wasn't alone, she saw him again as in her dream and knew that it was her duty to help him back to health and to whatever fate had in store for him, his work and the woman he loved. 'I've brought your flowers, Mr Wendover,' she said, softly. 'Shall I read the messages?'

'Another voice? Where's Sister?'

'I am Nurse Kavanagh. I'm going to be your special nurse, sir. There will be few changes now,' she said in a gentle voice.

'We'll see about that,' he said, and then his mouth hardened. 'Not the happiest of phrases, Nurse. You'll have to get used to me and bear with my bad temper.' He moved restlessly but kept his head on the pillow. 'Read the cards.'

Nuala read several messages, wondering at her own composure. He listened and half smiled. She read the one from Trudie. He laughed. 'There are two more small bunches of flowers,' she said.

'What did Trudie send?'

'Orchids and ferns and some small blue flowers. I don't know their name.'

'Gentians,' he said. 'That's what she would send.' He sighed. 'Can't you do something with this pillow?'

'It must be very boring for you to lie so low, but perhaps if I turned it, it will be cool.' She lost her own confused emotions in her trained discipline. 'Now hold on to my shoulder and let me take your weight while I slip the pillow over. Like so.'

His clutching hand slid away as she gently put his head back on the pillow. 'There's nothing of you, girl,' he said.

'I'm very strong,' she said. Oh, God, I'll have to be strong or I shall weep, she thought, but she read the last of the messages and tidied the table.

The next two days followed the same pattern. As soon as Nuala came on duty at eight in the morning, she popped in to say good morning to her new patient and then laid up the tray with sterile dishes and packs of sterile syringes and hypodermic needles in case Mr Micheljon needed to change the treatment and give injections other than the ones written up on the chart. On another tray were eye drops and sterile eyedroppers, soft cottonwool swabs and tiny towels to place beneath the patient's chin and cheek to catch any drops that might escape during instillation. Mr Micheljon was punctual, having other patients to see and sometimes a full list in the eye theatre.

The notice on the door handle was turned to DO NOT DISTURB, but Sister French knew from experience that some of the leading surgeons took it for granted that such notices were not meant for them if they felt like visiting a friend or a colleague who happened to be in the room. Her decision to place a nurse at the closed door to point out that the notice was intended for everyone was very wise, and twice, Nuala had tactfully to stand in the path of doctors who 'wanted to pop in for five minutes before doing a ward round'.

As soon as the bandage was back in place over fresh soft pads to shut out the light and not cause any pressure, Mr Micheljon would emerge and go with Sister French into her office to add notes to the chart and to fill her in with the latest news about her prize patient. Nuala's job was to clear the trays, tidy the bed and make sure that her patient was comfortable and to leave him alone if he needed a brief rest, even when he said rather testily that he wasn't a child and he was ready for breakfast.

'First, you have to be bathed, Mr Wendover,' she said, softly, and was glad that he couldn't see her smile. Even if his eyes were hidden, the rest of his face glared and he tried to sit up. 'Come on, now,' she pleaded. 'Do you want to get me into trouble with Sister?' Resignedly, he would lift a hand and let it fall to the bedcover and then grin. 'Will you tell me what to order for breakfast so that I can order it while I wash you?'

'I'm not hungry,' he said on the first two mornings, and he refused everything but toast and thickly-spread marmalade which he could manage without help, but on the third morning he asked for scrambled eggs and bacon. Nuala experienced a crazy desire to laugh and a quite illogical feeling of joy that he should accept the fact that he must eat even it meant having someone to feed him.

'You're feeling better,' she said, and went out to ring the diet kitchen. 'Could you make some fingers of toast covered with the scrambled egg so that he can help himself with just a little guidance?' she asked, and went back with the washing trolley. A junior nurse was on call to help with the bed-making and to arrange the pillows when Nuala turned her patient so that she could rub his back with spirit after washing and drying it carefully. At first, there had been a tense atmosphere and he was very embarrassed, but Nuala and the junior chatted while they attended to his needs so that he realised that to the average nurse this was nothing more than essential routine to be finished as quickly as possible, leaving him cool and refreshed and much more comfortable.

Outwardly this was so, but if she had been honest with herself, Nuala felt a little of his unease. She dismissed it as a natural reaction to having to nurse a surgeon, not having been in charge of such a high-powered member of staff who would know immediately if she put a foot wrong. 'Thank you, Nurse,' he said when the bed cover was in place and the pillows soft and tidy. 'It does make a difference,' he admitted. 'I can see now how important it is to train nurses to do these tasks well. I'm afraid that we often take it all for granted and think that anyone could do these duties.' He smiled. 'I'm certainly glad I haven't just anyone doing it for me. When I think of some of the, shall we say, heftier nurses, of my acquaintance, I suppose I might consider myself lucky to have your ministrations.'

The junior nurse chuckled. 'Is that a compliment, or are we the lesser of two evils, sir?'

Nuala waited for his reply. She couldn't believe that this was the same man who, only yesterday, had thrown down a bread roll on to the floor at lunch time when he picked it up by the buttery side. So he could be pleasant, as she had been told by everyone who came into contact with him in a professional capacity. But which was the real Blake Wendover? Was it the man who charmed his patients and was admired for his expertise, or was it the cool angry man who had been so unfair when his consulting room was untidy even when he must have known that all the staff had gone to lunch thinking that he had finished for the morning. His behaviour as a patient had not been angelic, either. She remembered the first day in his room when he grumbled that he couldn't get used to all the different voices and wanted to know who was supposed to be caring for him.

The door opened and Sister French came up to the bed, approaching on the right-hand side and standing a few inches from the bed so that she wouldn't touch it and startle him with a sudden jerk. She watched her staff nurse pin the large label to the bedcover, saying 'APPROACH THIS SIDE ONLY' and smiled. Over the years in the eye ward at St Jude's, this was established as a routine practice, so that patients with eyes bandaged knew that if someone wanted to speak to them or come with food or treatment, they would never creep up on the wrong side of the bed and so disturb or frighten them. Mr Wendover had grudgingly agreed that it was quite a good idea when it was explained to him.

'Mr Micheljon is very pleased with you,' Sister said. 'He said that the Atropine drops are working well and the inflammation is less. You can now have your antibiotics every eight hours instead of four-hourly.'

'That's a relief,' he said, but a pulse began to beat at the side of his mouth, showing the stress he suffered.

'I'll see if your breakfast is ready, Mr Wendover,' said Nuala, leaving Sister with the junior nurse, knowing that her patient would need nothing more until she came back with his tray. She also wanted to catch Sister French on her way back to the office so that she could speak to her without Mr Wendover hearing her. As with all people unable for one reason or another to see, the other senses had become acute and he was very sensitive to noise and voices and heard everything that was said in the corridor outside unless the people talking spoke in low voices.

Sister French seemed to know that Nurse Kavanagh wanted to speak to her and came out almost at once. 'Is everything all right, Nurse?'

'Fine, Sister. I think he's getting used to me now, after a rather shaky start the first day.' Sister laughed. 'There is one thing that I thought I ought to tell you, Sister. I noticed this morning that he licked his lips very often and seems to drink a lot of water. He complained of the central heating, saying it dried his mouth and that he hates dead air.' Nuala shrugged. 'He spends most of his working life in air-conditioning, in the theatre, special units and in the hotels where he lectures abroad, so this must be something fresh.'

'I'm glad you mentioned it, Nurse. Mr Micheljon has been giving him a rather concentrated solution of Atropine drops and for the first two days he came back at night to instil more. The dryness is caused by the Atropine. You know how you feel after taking a travel-sickness pill?' Nuala nodded. She had taken sickness pills only twice and she hated her reaction to them, feeling thirsty for at least a day after taking them.

'He'll have to continue the drops so that the pupil of the eye is dilated, resting the muscle, but if too much Atropine is absorbed and produces symptoms, we give Pilocarpine injections to stimulate the salivary glands. It keeps the mouth moist and there is no need to be continually drinking or feeling dry. I'll ring Mr Micheljon and you can prepare an injection for your patient as soon as I have the dosage prescribed.'

Nuala went back to her patient and set the tray on the bed table. The kitchen had prepared an attractive breakfast and she thought it was sad that he couldn't see it and appreciate the trouble that had been taken for him. The tray was far more carefully prepared than any other she had seen on its way into another room. News of his admission to the wing must have spread even to the diet kitchens and Nuala wondered with a secret smile who had the crush on him down there. The tiny posy of flowers on the napkin said it all.

'Someone put flowers on your tray.' He grunted. 'Shall I pour coffee now or would you rather wait until you have eaten something?'

'What is there? I don't want a cereal.'

'No cereal. Just what you ordered. Lovely

creamy scrambled eggs on fingers of toast with crispy bacon beside them.'

'How am I supposed to eat it?'

Nuala gently tucked the napkin under his chin and put a towel on the bed under his hand. 'Just take one like this. You can't make a mess, I've covered the sheet.' Her voice was soft and she guided his hand to the plate. 'I'll spear the bacon on the fork and when you want a mouthful, I'll pop it in.'

'I'm not a baby,' he grumbled, and took one of the fingers of toast from the plate when Nuala guided his hand towards it.

'No, you're not a baby,' she said, and he stopped eating for a moment, unsure of the inflection in her voice.

'You think I'm behaving badly, don't you, Nurse?'

'I'm sure I think nothing of the kind. I'd be very upset if I couldn't see,' she said, in a tone that was both sympathetic and bracing. 'Eat up before it gets cold. Try some bacon, it smells good.' She endeavoured to give him breakfast without his feeling too dependent on her help and as he held the coffee cup to drink and sipped it appreciatively, she knew that the simple change from using a flexible drinking tube to using a cup again made a lot of difference to his morale. Mr Micheljon had allowed him two pillows for mealtimes, enabling his head to be raised high enough to make drinking from a civilised cup quite easy.

'That was very good, Nurse.' The words came with some reluctance, but she knew what an effort it was for him to be pleasant and she made no comment but stowed the dirty crockery on to the tray, and put it on the shelf outside the door where the orderly could collect it. She brought a warm wet sponge and towel and told him that she was going to wipe his hands, before taking his right hand in hers and cleaning off a spill of bacon fat and marmalade. His hand was firm and the dark hairs on the back seemed to add to the picture of helpless power, a tiger caged or a perfect piece of machinery at rest without fuel. She saw how carefully his fingernails were tended and asked if he would like her to file away a tiny snag on the thumb nail.

He took the sponge from her and wiped his mouth. 'That's better,' he said, as if the refreshing tidying was all his idea. He let the sponge fall on the bed and she shook her head as she saw the small damp patch that formed on the coverlet before she could snatch it up again. He refused to let her touch his nails. 'I prefer to do them myself,' he said. I don't want you poking about under the nails and jabbing sharp points into me.'

'You have rather nicely-shaped fingernails, Mr Wendover. It would be a pity to see them get out of shape after all the care you have given them.'

'Under that soft, gentle and completely misleading voice, I suspect a will of iron, Nurse Kavanagh. I can't think why I have never seen you about the hospital. Where have you been hiding? You'll find a nail file and manicure set in my toilet bag, but I can't think that this comes within your work schedule.'

'Anything that helps the patient comes as part of the service,' she said demurely, but there was a lilt in her voice he had never noticed during their earlier exchanges. 'I haven't been back at St Jude's for a year, so it's unlikely that you have seen me.' She hoped that he wouldn't match the Nurse Kavanagh who was nursing him with the Nurse Kavanagh who was such a disgrace in Outpatients. With any luck, Sister Frazer hadn't mentioned her name to him or if she had, then he was too enraged to take it in at the time. Certainly, as he said her name, he was talking about a girl he had never seen.

Sister French opened the door and looked at the tidy room with approval. 'The flowers are ready to come in, Nurse.' She stood by the bed while Nuala wheeled in the silent rubber-tyred trolley and put vases of flowers on the window ledges, on the side table and on the bed table, out of reach of Mr Wendover should he grope towards it to search for his drinking glass or a fruit pastille. Everything he might want to find for himself, she put on the side locker and told him just where they were. Sister smiled. 'You're very lucky to have Nurse Kavanagh,' she said. 'She thinks of everything.' She laughed. 'I'll even let her give you your injection.'

'What injection?' The atmosphere in the room was suddenly tense and Sister French looked embarrassed.

'I'm sorry. I thought that Mr Micheljon might have warned you that if the Atropine began to give adverse symptoms, you would have to be given Pilocarpine.'

He relaxed. 'I'm sorry,' he said, flatly. 'I thought for a moment that I was for theatre.'

'We wouldn't have given you breakfast if you were about to have an anaesthetic,' said Sister.

'Nothing has been decided and of course we'd give you due warning of any change in treatment.'

'Pilocarpine? I should have thought of that. It's a strange sensation lying here, Sister.' He sank back into the pillows as if retreating from her. 'I am at your mercy. Even my thought processes have changed. If I was standing where you are, looking down at a bed patient, I would know exactly what was needed, but now, I am just another patient who can't make a self-diagnosis.'

'Just as well. More harm is done by doctors who think they know all about their own conditions than is done by the same men when they see patients.' Sister French put the small kidney dish on the bed table and showed the phial of Pilocarpine to Nurse Kavanagh for checking. She drew up the required amount of liquid into the syringe and pushed out the air bubble, leaving the injection ready to give.

'May I have your right arm, Mr Wendover,' said Nuala, and pushed the silk pyjama sleeve high. Sister French went away and closed the door after her. 'Would you like me to count to three before injecting?' said Nuala.

'No, just get on with it. Ouch!' With one swift movement, she had swabbed his arm with spirit and plunged the needle in. It was all over in a second. 'No messing about with you, Nurse Kavanagh. I must remember that when you intend doing something, it's as good as done. Are you as hard on all those boyfriends back home in Ireland?' His smile was forced again as if he resented being at a disadvantage and her heart sank. I thought we had crossed that barrier, she thought, he seemed quite glad to depend on me just now.

'Boyfriends? I'm dedicated to my career, Mr Wendover.'

'That I refuse to believe. Tell me, Nurse Kavanagh, didn't the good nuns or whoever educated you tell you that it's a sin to tell lies?' His mouth was mocking and she saw the lines that hinted at tension and sadness forming at the corners.

'I don't tell lies,' she said.

'Then tell me what you have heard? Am I to see again?' He seized her hand and pulled her roughly to the side of the bed. The manicure set that she was about to gather together as she finished the last nail slipped on to the floor.

'I don't know. Oh! you're hurting me.'

'She doesn't know.' He still held her hand, but now his strong fingers smoothed the back as if to soothe any pain he had caused her. 'At least that is honest. I think if you had said all the platitudes one expects, I would have sent you away for ever.'

'I thought you hated changes.' Her voice was low and she couldn't hide the quiver that showed how deeply she was touched. 'I would never tell you that everything was all right if it wasn't, and I would never relay anything told to me in confidence by Sister or Mr Micheljon, even if you tried to force it from me.'

He raised her hand to his lips. 'Such a tiny hand to be so strong,' he said. He made an effort to return to normal. 'And speaking of strong hands, can you lift down the suitcase from the top of the wardrobe?' He was once more the cool and rather cynical man she knew best, hating himself for showing any kind of weakness. He listened to the soft swish of her cotton dress and the almost silent

footsteps on the parquet by the door as she went to
get a chair on which to stand. 'Can't you reach it
without a chair?'

She blushed, forgetting that he couldn't see her
and pulled her skirt lower as she stood on the chair
and reached up to get the case. 'Did you mean the
small red one?'

'Is that there? I'd forgotten. Good, bring it down
and I'll get my secretary here tomorrow to take a
few letters in reply to the ones in the file there.'

'You can't do that. What would Mr Micheljon
say?'

The mouth was hard again and Nuala knew that
even if she looked back to this time from another
ten years she would know each change in his face,
each line of his mouth and each reluctant smile that
made it change to something of beauty and
humour. 'It has nothing to do with him.'

'Hasn't it though? If you take on too much just
now and it harms your chances of full recovery, it
would be very much his business.'

He lay back and to her surprise he laughed.
'Nurse Kavanagh. I had no idea that you were such
a bully. I have no idea what you look like, I know
nothing about you as a person in your own right
away from that absurd uniform they make you girls
wear, and yet you calmly tell me what I can or
cannot do.'

'It's for your own good,' she told him severely.

'Is it?' His voice was flat and tired.

'Yes it is,' she said, and the sweetness of the soft
Irish voice seemed to mend his smile.

'Pour me some orange squash,' he ordered. 'And
help me to drink it.' She poured about two inches

into the glass and held it to his lips, supporting his head on her arm. He drank and paused and she thought he was taking a new breath before drinking again, but his face turned and his lips brushed her bare arm.

She moved away, forcing herself to remain calm. 'Have you had enough?' she asked.

'For the moment.' His lips curled mischievously. 'You have soft rounded arms, Nurse, not the sticks I would have expected in one so tiny.'

'All muscle,' she said, lightly. 'I come of a wiry family.'

'Tell me about your family.'

'It wouldn't interest you, sir.'

'I think it would, but if you won't tell me, I'll tell you.' She moved about the room as if busy, hoping he would leave her alone. The man in bed dominated the room and she had to keep away from him. 'You went to a convent?'

'Yes. I went to school there.'

'The good sisters wanted you to join them?'

'To be a nun?' A bubbling laugh escaped her. 'I was far too bad for that.'

'A tomboy?'

'Of course. What else with three brothers and their friends? Living in the country we had to make our own amusements such as climbing trees and sailing.'

'You sail? A puff of wind would blow you overboard.'

'No it wouldn't.' She forgot to whom she was speaking. 'I'm good with boats. I sailed right across the Shannon on my own once, and not at the narrowest part.'

'A nurse, a guardian angel and a sailor. Well, well. With all that, you must be very beautiful.' She looked at him sharply, expecting ridicule but his mouth was at repose and he seemed to be poised in an agony of expectancy.

'Of course,' she said, airily. 'Very beautiful.' What did it matter? Long before he was better, she would have gone, either to another department or back to Ireland, if she changed her mind about marrying Dermot. 'I have fine blonde hair which I have cut carefully so that it forms a halo round my head. I have small features and a lovely red mouth and clear skin.' She laughed, trying to make him accept it as a joke. 'Shall I go on?'

'Please do.' He was listening intently.

'I've been told I have nice rounded limbs.' She looked at him expecting him to laugh.

'So other people noticed that, too?'

'Of course.' Silly man, or was he leading her on to make even more outrageous statements? 'I have small feet and hands, but you know that, and a small waist.' She frowned. It *was* true, all of it, but said as she had done, it was another girl. It was a girl without freckles and with hair cut by a professional and arranged with care. It was a girl with the appeal that made men's heads turn.

'Sounds good. I can't wait to see you for myself. One thing you forgot.'

'What was that?' Her mouth was dry as if she had been taking Atropine, and not her patient.

'Your voice. I had no idea how important a voice could be.' There was a tap on the door and Matron entered, on her way round the wing, making gracious visits to all but the very ill. 'Who the hell is that?' said Mr Wendover and the regal eyebrows shot up in pained surprise.

'It's Matron. It's the Superintendent of Nursing,' hissed Nuala.

'Ah, Matron, how good of you to call in.' The voice was bland again. 'I thought for a moment it was someone very boring who I didn't want in here.' Matron relaxed. 'I refused to have my telephone connected in here to avoid interruptions and I am having no visitors from outside at present.'

'I quite understand and I think you are being sensible. Nurse Kavanagh can take any messages for you. It might be a good idea if you dictated names of people you wish to contact you and as the calls come in, Nurse can vet them and let only the ones you wish to speak to personally, filter through.'

His tone changed to one of respect. 'That's a splendid idea. All calls can come to the wing but Nurse can plug in the phone here for the ones I put on the list.' Matron smiled, well satisfied, and left. 'Sorry about that,' he said. 'I'm afraid this makes me even more bloody-minded than usual.'

'I wouldn't say that,' Nuala said.

He seemed to be thinking hard. 'I'll decide what that means later,' he said. 'Can you take down the names now?'

'Only three people?' she asked as he stopped.

'Just my mother and a special colleague from my old hospital.'

'And Trudie l'Estrade.'

'Yes, Trudie.' A half smile touched his lips. 'I doubt if you, Matron or anyone could keep Trudie from talking to me if she had that intention.' He put out a hand for a drink. 'Most of my professional friends are in this hospital and they can get news through the usual grapevine and any others will hear soon enough about me.'

'Miss l'Estrade heard quickly.' Nuala bit her lip. The flowers had been ordered and flown from Italy and arrived as soon as Blake Wendover was admitted.

'I asked them to cable her,' he said. 'I should have met her in Geneva.' He shrugged. 'We had plans, but we shall have to postpone them. It's too bad.'

'Are you very disappointed?'

'What do you think? Would any man want to lie here like this when he could be in Switzerland looking at the white snow and the vivid blue sky and Trudie sweeping down the runs wearing an outrageous set of ski clothes?'

'Is she good on skis?' Her hand shook as she touched the gentians in the bouquet.

'Trudie is good at everything. She is very blonde and blue eyed, has the figure of a model and the skill of an athlete and laughs at everything.' He smiled as he remembered her, and Nuala was excluded from the world of the rich and self-possessed, the beautiful and fashionable. His world, and one into which she could never poke her freckled little nose. Not in a million years could she hope to take part in that world except as a spectator, and the sooner she realised that any light conversation between her and her august patient would lead to nothing but heartache for her and less than nothing for him, the sooner she could get on with her own plans for any future she could hope to have away from his magnetic aura.

'Do you think she'll telephone?'

'I don't know. Knowing Trudie, I think she might ring me up at dead of night, not knowing about a simple thing like date lines, or she might arrive here expecting the hospital authorities to let her treat the place like a hotel.' Nuala was fascinated and shocked. She sounded very unpredictable and not the kind of woman she could imagine living with Blake Wendover as a lifelong partner, but he was lying in bed with a silly, affectionate smile on his lips, obviously adoring the stupid woman and dreaming of the time when he could be with her. Nuala was ashamed and alarmed at the force of her own reactions to the idea of her patient being the slave of an empty-headed blonde. She knew it was no concern of hers and tried to think rationally about it. Mr Wendover was a strong healthy man with all the instincts that went with that condition. If he had never married, it must have been because he had never found time to do so, or had been satisfied with a string of girlfriends all willing and eager to fill his leisure hours. He would want to fall in love and marry someone spectacular. He needed someone who could be a sparkling hostess and stay beautiful and admired under any circumstances.

He was still smiling when she went to lunch, having tucked him in for a rest before eating his own lunch. Trudie l'Estrade would know people of many nations, be the perfect foil to his dark good looks, demand service and popularity wherever she went and give him love and the passion that a man like that would demand and give in return. Passion.

Nuala closed her eyes and almost collided with a trolley, receiving a dirty look from the porter wheeling it. What was she doing? How could she try to imagine herself in the place of the woman that Blake Wendover loved? But it was too late. I'm falling in love with him, and he will remember nothing about me in six months time.

CHAPTER FOUR

SOME of the flowers were faded and Nuala pulled them from the vases and wrapped them in newspaper she begged from a neighbouring room.

'What are you doing?' asked Blake Wendover. 'It's rather like having a quiet and busy little mouse rustling paper, or washing glasses.'

'I'm sorry if it disturbs you. Would you like me to take the flowers outside to sort them out? I can leave them for the orderly to do later when the flower trolley comes to collect them for the night, but these are so lovely, I enjoy arranging them and making sure they are fresh.' She laughed. 'And I think my efforts are rather more artistic than hers. There is a lot of pretty fern that has to be spread to show it off to the best advantage.'

'I'll take your word for it.'

Nuala bit her lip. It was so difficult to keep him interested in what was happening around him and she sensed that he liked to have someone in the room with him, but everything she mentioned was visual and she couldn't avoid saying things that emphasised his lack of sight.

'The scent of the carnations has lasted well,' she said.

'Full marks for trying,' he said. 'Is this an "appeal to the senses he has left" operation?'

She sighed and the sound was no more than the

whisper of a leaf, but he heard it. This was the fourth day and he lay like a wounded knight, the lines round his mouth deeper as each day passed and the bandages remained. 'You do like the scent, don't you?' she said.

'I like it. But don't sigh. I promise I'll be an ideal patient today. That wasn't the beginning of a good grumble.'

'You don't grumble, much,' she said. 'Is there anything you'd like before I go to lunch?'

'Come here.' She approached the bed, slowly. 'Give me your hand, Nurse Kavanagh.' She rested one hand lightly on the bedcover and he closed his strong fingers over it. 'I may be the world's worst patient, but I do appreciate all you are trying to do for me.' Her mouth quivered, but she managed to keep her hand from trembling. 'Forgive me if I bawl at you sometimes.'

She tried to take her hand away. 'It's an occupational hazard,' she said. 'I've yet to meet a surgeon who doesn't let off steam to his staff on occasion.'

His fingers held hers in a vice-like grip. 'You haven't said you forgive me,' he said. His mouth curved wickedly. 'Bend down. I have something very private to say.'

'Is it something you're wanting, sir? If so, you can speak up, because we are quite alone.'

'The walls have ears,' he said. His hand pulled her closer, with remorseless intent, and he sat up. Abruptly, his arms went round her and with commendable precision in one who couldn't see, his mouth found hers and she was kissed, firmly and expertly before being released.

'Mr Wendover! That was quite uncalled for. I

don't know what to do about you. Mr Micheljon said you were to lie flat for another day.'

He laughed and the sound was warm and deep and should have found an answer, but she was too confused and upset to do anything but stand away from the bed, twisting the edge of her apron in her hands. 'Is your name Kate?'

'No it is not.'

'A pity. What was it? That piece in Shakespeare? *Henry V*, I believe, when the king kissed Katherine for the first time, and she acted rather as you did then. You must remember.'

'I'm not well up in Shakespeare.'

'But you remember that. I heard that sharp intake of breath. How does it go? "There is witch-craft in your lips, Kate," or words like that.'

'And she replied that the tongues of men were full of deceits,' said Nuala, her temper rising.

'Ah, so you do know your Shakespeare. And have you found men deceitful, Kate?'

'My name isn't Kate.'

'Then how shall I call you?'

'I am on duty, Mr Wendover, and it is strictly forbidden for patients to address their nurses by any name but their second names.' How dare he treat her so lightly? He was in love with his heady blonde bombshell and yet he was prepared to amuse himself at her expense. And the price was too much. Nuala put a hand to her lips. They were soft and yielding, retaining the impress of his mouth and the memory of the shock wave of com-mitment that followed the contact. She stifled a sob.

His ears strained to hear her. 'I apologise,' he

said, stiffly. 'I was only saying thank you, but I can tell that it upset you. It won't happen again, Nurse Kavanagh.' His face relaxed again. 'But you have been very sweet you know. I'm very lucky to have you to look after me. Please don't let this alter anything.'

'Of course not.' She swallowed deeply and smiled. The damage was done, but he couldn't know that. He would never guess that the kiss so lightly given had sealed her fate for the future. If Dermot still wanted her, she might as well marry him. After all, she had been fond of him at one time and they got on well together when he was in a good mood. No man could have the same effect on her as this man lying between the white sheets, his eyes bandaged and his heart in torment in case his sight was lost for ever. He would never know it, but her heartache would be her gift to him of service and caring for as long as he needed it.

If he was blind, permanently? She shuddered, but one corner of her mind didn't grieve. If he was blind, he would need someone to look after him and he was used to having her near, knowing what he wanted almost before he knew it himself and smoothing the day for him. She touched the fading gentians and then tore them from the vase. Trudie didn't sound the type to care for a blind man. She would want to travel and socialise, to be seen in all the smart resorts and to follow her own desires. So many sports would be impossible for him and Trudie wouldn't sit and watch others when she wanted to hurtle down the difficult Alpine runs. Nuala touched his hand. 'I'm going to lunch now,' she said.

Sister Odinga was just in front of her in the line for food in the cafeteria when Nuala arrived late for lunch. 'How's my favourite man, or my second favourite? I suppose I must put my man first, but Blake Wendover is special.'

'You think so?'

'You should know. You must know him better than most after looking after him for five days.'

'Four days,' said Nuala.

'Well, most of the staff would be delighted to look after him. What's wrong? Bad news from home?'

'No, in fact, I had a very impassioned letter from Dermot wanting to name the day.'

'Well, cheer up, then. If that's what you want, you should be bubbling over.'

'Bubble, bubble,' said Nuala, glumly.

'Is it Blake? He isn't going to be blind?' The warm brown eyes filled with tears. 'Oh, no, it couldn't happen to him.'

'They don't know what will happen. Mr Micheljon saw him this morning and was cautiously pleased, but the possibility of him having a laser seal to the retinal detachment is looming up.'

'So there is a detached retina?'

'Definitely in one eye and the other is inflamed but probably just in sympathy with the other.' Anxiety for the physical condition of her patient made a useful shield behind which she might hide her true feelings and sadness. 'He isn't very happy but he tries to hide it. Tell me, has he a reputation for chatting up the nurses?'

Sister Odinga raised her eyebrows. 'I don't believe it. You aren't trying to tell me he made a pass at you?'

'No, he hasn't done that.' In all honesty, she couldn't accuse him of anything more than that one kiss given out of loneliness or real gratitude.

'It wouldn't fit in with my image of him,' said Odinga, firmly. 'Half the nurses at St Jude's have suffered sleepless nights lusting after him at one time or another, but he seems too busy and preoccupied with work to date any one person for more than a dinner date or a visit to the theatre if he has spare tickets. Everyone wonders if he will fall in love and marry, but so far there hasn't been a whisper about him and a special woman.'

'I think he spreads his net further than St Jude's. He had a beautiful bunch of flowers from Italy, flown over by a woman who was to have met him in Geneva.' Nuala felt the need to tell someone so that there would be no doubt that he was interested in someone outside the hospital, and she could never be accused of having an interest in him above that of his loyal and hard-working nurse. 'Naturally, he's disappointed that he can't meet her. She sounds as if she's very beautiful, very suitable for him and I think he's in love with her.'

'Tell yourself that often enough and you'll believe it,' said Odinga. 'Even if you are going to marry Dermot, I defy you to tell me that there isn't just a little something, a tiny frisson, when you make his bed.'

'That's absurd. We don't fall for every good-looking male patient. I've been nursing for three and a half years and I haven't fallen in love with a patient yet, and this is no time to start, if I'm to be married soon.'

Sister Odinga smiled and helped herself to a bread roll and butter to eat with her soup and salad. Nuala absent-mindedly took two and left her bowl of soup on the counter. 'Wake up,' said Odinga. 'You've forgotten your soup and you haven't decided what you want to eat after that.'

Nuala took an individual cottage pie and they found a table away from the door to the kitchen, which swung to and fro during the whole lunch break as kitchen staff pushed through with trolleys, clearing tables and stacking soiled trays. The food was better at St Jude's than at some of the hospitals where Nuala had worked or visited, but any institutional food has its limitations and becomes boring with repetition. The selection for lunch was predictable and seldom varied. Odinga sighed. 'I'm dying for a meal outside. Are you free tonight? We could go to that Chinese place that opened a few weeks back. I hear it's quite good.'

'I'd love to, but I have to be on duty for a while late at night to make him comfortable. I have every afternoon off while he naps and there is no nursing treatment due.'

'That gets boring.'

'I don't mind. I have more time to look at the shops and do my laundry and I even bought some material to make a summer dress.' Nuala glanced up at the grey sky that darkened the dining room so much that lights were on in the middle of the day. 'This weather makes me think that summer will never come.' She tore a piece off her first roll and buttered it. 'What date is it?'

'Getting on in March. Sixth or seventh?'

'I didn't know we were into March, but time flies so here.'

'Even stuck in one room with a man who does nothing for your libido?' said Odinga in a mocking voice.

'Even there.' Nuala refused to be goaded into saying something indiscreet. 'He has lovely flowers and I like arranging them. He takes up a lot of time as he is very restless and the bed looks like a tip about an hour after we've made it.'

'When will he know what's happening?'

'Nobody says much but I think Mr Micheljon is bringing another surgeon down from London for a second opinion before he risks a laser.'

'But that might not be for days. When do you have a day off?'

'I hadn't thought of that. I suppose I'm due for one, but I can't say I'm keen to leave him to another nurse for just a day.'

'That's ridiculous. He'll have to put up with it. Surely you've looked at the off-duty roster in Sister's office?' Sister Odinga seemed more remote and she spoke in her professional voice. 'You must have your off-duty. It's bad for you and in a way it's not good for your patient if you have a fixation for him.'

Nuala blushed. 'There's no chance of that. I'll look as soon as I get back.'

'I'm off tomorrow and I've tickets for that new musical in London. If you're interested, we could take an early train, have lunch and browse through Oxford Street before going to the theatre and taking the last train back.'

'I'd like that, but he'll be cross. He hates changes of staff.'

'Rubbish. He's lucky to have a special when he isn't in pain or really ill as far as bodily incapacity is concerned. If he was in the eye ward he'd be in a dark side ward with three other patients and have changes of care every day.'

'But he isn't an ordinary patient,' said Nuala, miserably.

'If you feel sorry for him, weep in private and never let him see that you are doing him a favour. Have your off-duty and be objective as far as you can. I know it's difficult, but he'll have to do without you at some time, and, what's more important, you'll have to do without him.' The gentle eyes were full of understanding. 'Have that day off and get yourself back in line. You owe it to yourself and there must be no hangups when you are married to Dermot.'

Quite good sponge pudding with orange sauce followed the cottage pie and Nuala had a second helping. 'At least I don't have to worry about putting on weight. I wish I could put on a few pounds. Mr Wendover was quite surprised that my arms weren't like sticks as I'm so small, but I could do with a curve or two.'

'He noticed that much about you?'

'Only when I made his bed. He has developed an acute sense of hearing and touch and can now tell how big a person is when they enter the room. He says he can tell the air displacement. I think he must be joking.'

'Maybe not. I once nursed a double cataract and while his eyes were bandaged, he said he had the same feeling.' Odinga laughed. 'We wrote DOM on the bottom of his chart to warn the other nurses about him.'

'DOM. What's that?'

'Dirty old man,' said Odinga, cheerfully. 'He would listen for us to come into the room and say he wanted to guess who we were. We stayed quiet and while we made the bed he guessed our names. But he had to wait until one of us held him up for the pillows to be arranged. He clutched as hard as he could, often in the wrong places, and announced his verdict.' She laughed. 'He was never wrong. He said he recognised the other nurse by her pillowy chest and me by my nice shoulder blades. He went a bit far sometimes and we sent a male nurse and the porter in to him. His face was a picture when he clutched two hefty men instead of a nice armful of nurse.'

'At least I shan't have that trouble,' said Nuala. After her shocked reaction to his kiss she wondered if he would want her to touch him again. A day off now might give him time to get back to their easy relationship, and when she went back to the wing to collect her bag she looked at the off duty list. Odinga was right. Her day off was tomorrow and a nurse had been told to take her place for the day. Fortunately, the nurse was working on the private patient wing and there was time to tell her about her new patient when Nuala came back on duty for the evening.

'He hates the telephone at present,' she explained. 'There are only three people who are to be put through to him if they call. The calls come to me first from the operator and I take messages, a bit like a secretary, and if he wishes to talk, I plug in the phone by his bed.' She went over the rest of her duties and then saw that the red light above his door was showing. He might not be able to see the time but he knows I'm late, she thought, and hurried into the room.

More flowers had arrived and lay on the table waiting to be arranged. As she had plenty of time to spare if Mr Wendover needed nothing, Nuala had offered to see to all his flowers to spare the overburdened nurse detailed to tend the mass of blooms that flowed in every day for the patients. In fact, when she knew that her charge was dozing or wanted to be quiet, she would slip out and do some flower arranging for the other rooms.

'Isn't the scent wonderful?' she said, taking up a bunch of freesias and holding them close to the bed.

'A little too heavy for me,' he said. 'Where have you been?'

'Off duty this afternoon, as usual.'

'It seemed a long time.'

'You had a nap, I hope?' She turned away with the flowers. 'Would you prefer violets near to the bed? These are beautiful. I think I ought to put the heads under water tonight to make sure they last a long time. My grandmother did that to violets and all violas from her garden. It's amazing how they lifted their heads the next day instead of hanging limp.' She chatted about the flowers and other trivia. He had missed her. She couldn't tell him that he would have to miss her for a whole day. It's just selfishness, she thought and hardened her heart. He was so used to getting his way in everything. People jumped to do his bidding, and students trailed after him on the wards and in the lecture room, hanging on every word, so it was inevitable that he should take it for granted that his nurse would be there at all times, seven days a week.

'Who sent the violets? I expect it was my mother. She does that to her violas, too, as she says they don't have a long vase life.'

Nuala looked at the card. 'It says "with much love from Mattie".' Not another woman hopelessly in love with him? When she read out some of the cards bearing extravagant messages, he just grunted and dismissed them with an impatient wave of his hand, but this time, he smiled.

'Put them close to me, Nurse. That is my mother.' She smiled, finding his pleasure infectious. 'You think I'm stupid having a mother who lets me call her Mattie?'

'No, why should I? Lots of people have pet names for relatives.'

'You were smiling. No, don't start like that. I can't see you, but I know your moods as you know mine.' He put out a hand to touch the violets that came cool and damp to his fingers. 'My mother's name is Matilda and she hates it. We all called her Mattie from childhood and she accepts it.'

'You are very good friends,' Nuala said, impulsively.

'Yes, we are. My father is dead and Mattie is very independent. She runs her own business and could be mistaken for my older sister. Many people have made that mistake.'

'Does she look like you?'

'They say so but I think she is beautiful.' He laughed. 'She also loves violets. I expect she bought at least six bunches for herself when she ordered these for me.' He smiled and seemed lost in thought, and Nuala brought a small shallow bowl into which the violets fitted well. 'I'll have them on my locker,' he said. Nuala couldn't help wondering why he wanted flowers from his mother close to his bed when he had not made any suggestion that the flowers sent by the woman he loved should be brought closer. Never once had he asked if the flowers that Trudie l'Estrade sent every day were lasting well or if they were beautiful. She frowned. Yesterday, he had insisted that the whole of that day's batch from whatever source should be sent down to the geriatric ward to please the old people who hardly saw flowers unless other patients sent them down to the ward.

'Even the ones from Italy?' Nuala had asked.

'All of them,' he answered, impatiently, and now he was selecting one bunch of humble violets to take the place of honour by his bedside.

'I think you'd like Mattie,' he said. 'She has a warped sense of humour.' He laughed as if at a secret joke.

'That's reassuring,' said Nuala, dryly. 'I don't know if I'd agree with you. I like less high-powered ladies.'

'That's good.' He laughed. 'I must tell her that she is high-powered.'

'That's not fair. I've never met the lady and I doubt if I shall meet her and I'd rather you didn't laugh at me.'

He turned towards her. 'Sometimes I want to tear off these bandages and see your face. At this moment, I suspect it is rather cross and those lovely eyes are flashing fire at me. Are you blushing, Nurse Kavanagh?'

'I never blush,' she said, blushing furiously.

'You told me you never tell lies,' he said. 'My mother has a peculiar idea about her future wife.'

'She has? Let me guess. She will have to be beautiful?' he nodded. 'Competent and as high-powered as she is?' He laughed. 'Well, all mothers have the same idea. And I suppose she thinks that no woman is good enough for her son? Has she met your intended wife?'

'Not yet. She has this dream that the woman will look beautiful with a face rather like a drenched violet, vulnerable and sweet but with inner strength.'

'And she's given up hope of you producing her and has to make to do with sheer beauty and all the social graces that someone like Miss l'Estrade can bring you.' Never in this world could Trudie look like a drenched violet, that was certain, even without meeting the dynamic lady.

'I bow to my mother's taste when I want new curtains, but I choose my own women,' he said, quietly. 'As for Miss l'Estrade, you may see her soon. She sent a cable to tell me she may be in England some day this week.'

'Tomorrow?' said Nuala, sharply.

'I have no idea. I hope not as I have to see another eye surgeon tomorrow. That will take all my attention.'

The telephone rang. 'Who plugged it in?' said Nuala. 'Do you want to answer it?'

'No, you answer it. I did take one call, but Sister forgot to take it away while you were off duty.'

'Nurse Kavanagh for Mr Wendover,' she said.

'Is that you, Nuala?'

'What do you mean by ringing me here? I'm on duty.' Nuala tried to speak softly but was aware that every word she said could be heard by the man in bed.

'I thought it was too good to be true,' said Dermot, carelessly, 'but as soon as I mentioned your name they put me through to you.'

'I am answering calls for Mr Wendover. That's the only reason you were connected. I can't take personal calls on duty.'

'But I'm here and I want to see you. Maureen couldn't put me up and I've taken a room in a small hotel outside the town.'

'Give me the telephone number and I'll ring you.'

'I want to see you tonight.'

'That's impossible. I'm not off duty until late.'

'Late would be fine.' His voice told her that he was laughing, sure of his hold over her, but he told her his number. 'See you soon, me darling,' he said as she put down the receiver.

'I'm sorry about that. The operator must have thought the call was for you.' She unplugged the telephone and put it outside the door on the shelf and plugged it in to the power there.

'You could have taken the call, Nurse Kavanagh. It sounded important.'

'Not at all,' she said.

'It was to him.' The mouth was set in an enigmatic line. 'He is in love with you?'

'Yes, he is, or so he says.'

'You don't sound sure.'

'He wants to marry me. I've known him all my life.' The lines on the face deepened. 'We grew up together and it has been expected that we shall marry one day.'

'Be very sure that you love him, Nuala.'

'How did you know my name?' His interest in Dermot wasn't important.

'I use my ears and some of the nurses in the corridor do shout sometimes when Sister isn't about.'

'I see.'

'It's a pretty name. A pretty name to go with a pretty face.'

'No.' It was a whisper. 'I'm not pretty.'

'You said you were beautiful.'

'I was teasing you because you wanted to know what I looked like. I'm very ordinary.'

'The man on the telephone. He doesn't think you ordinary, to come all the way from Ireland to see you.'

'You heard?'

'He was speaking loudly, against the noise in a bar, I think.'

'I'll telephone him later,' she said, to stop further questions. 'Is there anything I have to do to prepare you for your visitor tomorrow? You aren't due for more Pilocarpine today and Mr Micheljon said he would leave you tonight.'

'They will assess my condition tomorrow and decide if I'm to have surgery.' He bent sideways to catch the scent of the violets. 'I doubt if they will do anything for a few more days, but I have to make up my mind that what they offer, I must take.'

She wanted to go to him and cradle his head in her hands, to kiss the pads over his poor eyes and to soothe him. He needs a wife or mother to comfort him, she thought, and could imagine neither of the women in his life filling that need.

'Go on arranging the flowers. I like the sounds you make,' he said. Was he being polite to hide his own mental stress? His face seemed relaxed and somehow pleased. He needs nobody, she decided. He is strong enough to stand alone. He needs neither his mother or even Trudie to comfort him. It was a relief to know that he wasn't besotted with his mother, even if he loved her dearly. She shivered. Oedipus had loved his mother and blinded himself in guilty rage. Another man of immense power. She saw the firm lines of his face and the taut cords in his throat. This was no Oedipus. When he took a wife or a lover, she would know he was very male and had no Freudian hangups.

'Shall I read the other cards?' she said. He nodded and she read aloud, stacking the small bundle to put with the others in a drawer so that his secretary could take them and reply to the kind messages, on his orders. 'There seem to be more than ever as people get to know where you are,' she said.

'Flowers and fruit enough to set up a stall. Will you join me and take the money while I beat the drum?' he said.

'I'm not the type,' she said. 'I can't add up.'

The rest of the evening went by peacefully, with Blake Wendover talking about St Jude's and the staff, other hospitals he knew and gave a graphic description of the man coming to see him the next day. Nuala suspected that he wanted to keep his mind away from the ordeal of being examined by a fresh surgeon, and the sound of his own voice made him more confident.

'It's time you went off duty,' he said, at last.

'How do you know?' It was uncanny how easily he judged time when there wasn't even a striking clock in the area. 'I've plenty of time,' she said. 'I want to leave everything straight for tomorrow as I shall be off duty.' She sensed the stiffening in his manner. 'I was told to take tomorrow. I would prefer to stay and be here when they come to see you.' There was pleading in her voice and he smiled. 'Is there anything I can get when I go shopping?' she said. 'I think you need more toothpaste. Do you always use that brand?'

'Surely you will have too much to do tomorrow, now that your friend is here from Ireland?'

'I have to go shopping,' she said, 'And I am going to London with Sister Odinga to the theatre.'

'But surely, a woman in love would rush to her sweetheart's side and cancel all other dates?'

'I never cancel appointments unless I'm ill,' she said, firmly.

'Efficient, sweet and now a stickler for truth and honesty.' Was there derision in his voice, or reluctant admiration? 'I have a feeling that you still bear the marks of the nuns' training, Nurse Nuala.' He settled down in the bed. 'Have fun and don't make any hasty decisions,' he said. She stared at him. Did blindness lend him the power of extrasensory perception? How could he know what an important decision waited for her when she met Dermot?

'I never make hasty decisions,' she said, gravely. How was he to know that the sound of Dermot's voice had only strengthened her resolution and that she was determined to send Dermot away for ever? 'You haven't told me if you have any shopping for me to do.'

'I could use some more of the same toothpaste and perhaps some aftershave and a thing of talc that doesn't smell like washing-up liquid.'

'Anything more?' She giggled. The talc to which he had taken a dislike had been given him by a sister who had cherished a passion for him for a long time.

'Yes, I want a present for a lady. Buy some really expensive perfume. You choose it. Sometimes you wear something light and flowery when you come back from your time off. I think she'd like something similar. Nothing too heavy.' He insisted that she take a generous amount of money from his wallet and added several other small items to the list. 'Only bother with these if you can spare the time, and take Sister Odinga somewhere for a meal. I'm a great fan of hers.' It was impossible to refuse his offer. He wasn't giving her a treat and she had no right to refuse on behalf of the other woman, but must go along with the arrangement.

'I'm sure she'll be pleased, Mr Wendover.'

'I hope you both have a good time,' he said, politely. 'Make sure you have a good meal. You need fattening up.'

'I'm one of the lean kind.' But he had bothered to include her and she couldn't help being delighted. When she picked up the telephone and dialled the number that Dermot had given her, she was smiling, and it had nothing to do with the man from Ireland.

CHAPTER FIVE

'ARE you sure that you don't want to be with Dermot?' Sister Odinga looked anxious.

'I wouldn't have left it until we were in London to tell you about him if I had any doubts about coming with you today,' said Nuala firmly.

'He's come all this way and you saw him for just half an hour last night? How long will he be staying?'

'Dermot has to see someone to do with his course in architecture, so he wasn't here just because I happened to be at St Jude's. He has to meet the man today and I told him I had shopping to do for a patient and was meeting someone for a meal this evening, so he couldn't ask me to change my arrangements.'

'If he wanted your company badly, he could have followed you around after your shopping was over and he'd finished his appointment. Something tells me that this affair is lukewarm,' Nancy Odinga said.

'I am very fond of Dermot as a friend, but I know that I could never marry him. Once, when all the family took it for granted that it would happen, I thought it was inevitable, but I never thought much about the physical side of marriage until the day he tried to seduce me.'

'Put you off? I hope it only put you off marrying

him. All men aren't like that, and you have the kind of mouth that needs love. I can't think how men don't see it. They must be blind.' Sister Odinga looked stricken. 'That wasn't the best remark to make, was it?' She smiled. 'Come on, let's forget work and patients and lovers and be women out on a shopping spree. I love choosing perfume and you say that he wants you to buy the best.'

'He seemed vague about it. I hope I get what he likes. He was very caustic about the talc he was given. He wants something light and flowery and feminine. If it's for his lady-love, I think he's making a big mistake. Trudie l'Estrade sounds as if she would wear overpowering stuff. She sounds overpowering even without perfume. Can't think that she's the subtle perfume type.'

'So we get what the man ordered.'

They went into a famous London store and found the perfumery counter. After trying several different ones on every available patch of bare skin on wrists and forearms, Odinga said she smelled like a flower shop and couldn't smell any fresh scents. They wandered round and came back to the counter and tried two that both of them had liked, deciding on one that Nuala, in particular, would have liked to buy for herself, but when she saw the small bottle so highly priced, she knew that it was too expensive to consider. It was carefully wrapped and looked very attractive in the thick striped paper. The other items for Blake Wendover took very little of their time and they made their way to a smart coffee bar to recover and to watch London through the fake Dickensian windows.

'I'm glad I came,' said Nuala. 'You were right. I

can see St Jude's in perspective now that I am away from work.'

'And away from Blake? He has had an influence on you, whether you like to admit it or not.'

'Every patient has some influence on one's way of thinking, I suppose,' said Nuala, evasively. 'Being with him for so many hours a day does rather concentrate my attention on him.'

'When do you finish specialling him? He isn't all that bad, is he? No danger of depression or self-injury if left alone?'

Nuala looked startled. 'You don't believe he could act like that?'

'No, that's why I can't think how he managed to get a nurse all to himself after his pain had gone and his infection was cleared. Unless . . .'

'Unless Mr Micheljon knows more than he's telling us?' Nuala was pale. 'Do you think he's worse than they say and that he has no hope of regaining his sight?'

'Not at all,' said Odinga, calmly. 'I think he asked for a special nurse and is paying for that service as it doesn't come under necessities for which, as a consultant, he would pay nothing.'

'But why? He has masses of friends who are anxious to visit him and he sends vague messages that he'll send them invitations soon. There is no need for him to be alone for five minutes of the day if all he wants is someone to talk to him. I do very little, now. He insists that the night staff bath him as he likes to sleep a little before breakfast, and apart from making his bed umpteen times a day because he is so untidy, I do the flowers, deliver messages and hover, waiting for him to spill something, or to feed him.' She laughed. 'Once or twice, I've sloped off to help in the semi-private six bedder, because they really are busy there, but he gets cross if I'm away for long periods.'

Odinga shrugged. 'If he's paying, he wants his due.'

'But that's unfair. If he doesn't need me, he's preventing me from going where I really might be of use. How selfish can you get?'

'I don't know, but don't be too hard on him. He is in darkness and he hates it.'

'I know, but if he has to accept the fact that his sight might not be . . . perfect, he'll have to come to terms with it, as others have done.'

'Perhaps he thinks you might be willing to be his own private nurse if that happened.'

Nuala looked very upset and Odinga changed the subject and managed to get the girl to smile again.

The day passed quickly and they found a good eating house where they devoured steaks and baked potatoes, followed by apricot pie and thick cream. 'I shall go to sleep in the theatre if I eat any more,' said Nuala. They had been careful to order only one glass of wine each to drink with the meal because Nuala wanted to introduce her friend to Irish coffee as she had never tasted it. They sat in the lounge with the glasses before them and Nuala showed her how to pour the thick cream over the back of a silver spoon so that it floated on the surface of the coffee laced with Irish whiskey and brown sugar. Odinga looked up and wiped a band of white cream from her lips, her eyes sparkling. 'It's great,' she said. 'Such a strange mixture of ice-cold cream and hot coffee coming through it, with the warmth of the spirit giving a different feeling.'

They found their seats in the theatre, and in the swirling music and the beautiful gowns on stage, Nuala lost herself for a time, indulging in fantasies that she was beautiful and graceful and could lure men to their doom. In the darkness she sat and watched the brightness of the stage and thought of her meeting with Dermot. He was certainly handsome, rather like the man on stage who was singing and looking into the face of the heroine, smiling and making many girls in the audience wish that they could change places with the girl in the soft blue dress who gazed at him so adoringly. Yes, Dermot was quite a dishy man. Nuala frowned. His attitude last night was different. At home, he had insulted her by hinting that she was unattractive and frigid and so he had no further use for her, but now, he didn't even grumble when she said she could meet him for a drink in the local inn where he was staying, but couldn't see him on her day off.

It wasn't the relieved acceptance of a man who didn't really want her company but would put up with it because it was expected of him. This was more caring and that wasn't a bit like Dermot, who took everything for granted and expected all females to jump to his bidding.

The man on stage turned to see what effect he was having on the audience and although he could have seen little but a blur of faces over the footlights, the vibrations must have been good for he smiled with triumphant vanity. Nuala smiled. Just like Dermot, who could be very theatrical at times. Perhaps I am frigid, she thought. I didn't react to

Dermot's overtures in the way that most girls would have done and I haven't attracted many boys since I left school, so perhaps I am not cut out for marriage and children. I don't even feel a thrill when this handsome man pours out his love in song, and looks so delightful.

Last night Dermot had ordered drinks and steered her towards a corner table from where they could watch the comings and goings of others in the lounge. Nuala had recognised one or two people from the hospital, including, to her surprise, the junior nurse on the private patients' wing, with one of the medical students.

'Do you know him?' said Dermot, when the couple waved to her.

'I know the girl. She works on the private wing and I see the man sometimes when he's with a consultant in one of the clinics.'

Dermot regarded her solemnly. 'When are you coming home, Nuala?' It wasn't said accusingly, but rather sadly. 'I made a fool of myself once, but surely you wouldn't hold that against me for ever?'

'No, I don't bear you any ill will, Dermot, but it did help me to make up my mind. I thought of you a lot when I was here, doing my training, and I suppose that habit made me take it for granted that we would be married after I finished training. I enjoyed seeing you during the holidays and hoped that you enjoyed meeting me.'

'I did, and I do. Can you look at it from my side? I felt as you did and then I found that there were girls more ready to have a bit of fun and who were more, well, were a bit more developed than you. It made me think I needed time to see the world before I settled down. Is that a sin?'

'It's no sin to see the world, Dermot, but if you think I could marry you after you'd had your fill of loose living, then you're very much mistaken,' she said, crisply. 'When you . . . after that evening when we quarrelled, I knew I didn't want to marry you and I still feel the same.'

He sipped his stout and looked sad. 'It's so unfair. We quarrelled and I saw another Nuala, with some of the old temper I liked when we were children. You really let yourself go and you looked different. As I was losing you, it was then that I really began to love you.'

She looked down at her hands. 'I felt so angry,' she said.

'Then, you'll come home and forget that silly incident?' He leaned forward and she saw the excitement in his blue eyes.

'No, I'm not ready to come back yet. I have an important case to look after and I don't know how long it will take.' Why did she think that Dermot was too eager, like a man trying to sell her expensive insurance and afraid that his customer might back out at the last minute?

Dermot leaned back. 'But you will come back.' It was a statement. 'It doesn't matter if you aren't ready now. Everything takes time to organise and when we are married we want everything comfortable and as we like it.'

'I haven't said I'll marry you, Dermot. As I feel now, that's the last thought in my mind, but I hope we can be good friends.' She smiled and watched his self-confidence ooze away under his brightness.

'You do love me.' He said it with force as if to imprint the message on her mind. 'You do love me because you know me and we have always been close. It's fine to feel a little independent, but it's time we settled down.'

'Let's talk of home and enjoy our drinks. I'm not going to argue with you, Dermot. I've had a busy day and I'm tired.'

At once, he was concerned and attentive and she was even more confused. Did he love her? Had he made that discovery, as he said, because she showed more spirit and was flushed with anger? Nuala knew that since that time she had matured in her outlook. She had been forced to grow up and face her future, a future possibly alone, working hard all her life in a world of self-sacrifice and service. Perhaps that maturity made her more attractive.

He had walked back to the hospital with her through the fresh night and had kissed her when they reached her door. This kiss was warm and gentle, more passionate than the ones he used to leave hovering between lips and cheek, and less bold than the ones to which he had subjected her on the beach and on the hillside. In spite of herself she was stirred to respond. If he could be like this, she could be comfortable with him and even find a mild degree of happiness, but in the back of her mind was the picture of the man with the bitter corners to a full and beautiful mouth, and eyes that couldn't look at her with any expression, not even indifference—and Dermot was nothing.

He seemed well satisfied, however, and walked away whistling a jaunty tune that made her think of home. The niggling sense of something wrong clung to her as she went to bed and it was only now, sitting in the darkness of the theatre that she had time to consider it again.

'Are you enjoying it?' whispered Odinga. 'I love the dancing.'

'It's great,' said Nuala, who wasn't conscious of seeing the past fifteen minutes.

'Have we time for coffee afterwards?'

'If we get out first,' said Nuala. 'There's a café near the theatre that has quick service.' She wondered what Dermot was doing after his business meeting. Perhaps he was seeing other friends while he was in town. I haven't heard from Mother lately, she thought, and resolved to check her letter slot in the lodge of the block of flats and bedsitters.

'When do you see Dermot again?'

'Tomorrow. I have the afternoon off again, as usual, and we can walk by the river or over the Downs, if it doesn't pour with rain. March is such an unpredictable month. I never know what to wear, but at least I've had my hair well cut.'

'It suits you. You'll have to keep it up now and go down the road to the man near the hospital. He's very good. My hair is thick and very wiry, but he manages to make it lie flat and to move in the right way.'

'I'll make an appointment soon and maybe have a light perm. It needs more body,' said Nuala recklessly.

'All for Dermot?'

'Certainly not. I think I look better on duty and I feel better without all those ends.'

'You aren't hoping to make a good impression on

your patient as soon as he can see?' said Odinga.

'No, I am *not*,' said Nuala, crossly. 'It's time I had a new look. In any case, his beautiful girlfriend might be coming to see him this week. If he had four eyes, they would all be for her. I am just the mouse who arranges his flowers and rubs his back.' She paused. 'Or I was. He doesn't let me do that any more. Not that he's said as much, but he manages to have all that done by the night staff and I just swan around as if I never heard of anything so vulgar as a bedpan or a bed bath.'

'You must be bored, doing nothing all day.'

'No, he keeps me busy, but I couldn't say how. I read to him, sometimes. He likes that.'

'Poor Nuala. Do you have to plod through all the medical journals?'

'No. Yesterday I had to read poetry and the day before it was *The Wind in the Willows*.' She giggled. 'He asked me to choose and I found a copy in the waiting room.'

'But the poetry was his choice?'

'We've time for another cup of coffee. Shall I get them?' Nuala couldn't tell her friend how shaken she had been when he asked her to read love poetry. Her voice had shaken as she read the beautiful words of Omar Khayyám,

'Ah Love! Could thou and I conspire
 To grasp this sorry scheme of things entire,
 Would we not shatter it to bits . . . and then
 Remould it nearer to our heart's desire?'

He had been silent and still until she went on to a more cheerful piece, but her heart ached to do just that: to put the clock back and remodel his life as it should be, with perfect sight, the return to his old pride and arrogance, even if it meant that he would never see her, never touch her and would never have met her. Even in jest, he would never have kissed her.

'We ought to hurry. It's later than I thought,' she said, and they hurried out, buttoning their coats against the cold March wind.

The letter slot was empty again and Nuala frowned as she went to her room. As far as she knew there had been no postal strikes and the service was good. If I don't hear from home tomorrow, I'll telephone, she thought. Perhaps there was another crisis. Her cousin Maureen was pregnant and she might be ill. Nuala wondered if she should write to her, but if Maureen was over the sick stage, she ought to be in good health. I might be difficult to contact, being late on duty each evening. If my family rang, I'd still be on duty and unobtainable, she thought. There was a slight feeling of guilt, knowing that she stayed far longer than necessary, convincing herself that the water jug needed changing, the flowers should be sorted out to help the night staff and the orange squash should have ice in it. The intimacy and peace of the room, with her relaxed patient, the sound of his voice and the occasional touch of his hand was enough to make her stay for as long as she dared.

The room was warm and Nuala was glad to be back in the comparative peace of the Downs. She smiled as she went to bed, wondering how his temper had reacted to a day with a fresh nurse.

It was with a sense of urgency that she went on duty the next morning, in crisp clean clothes and freshly-washed hair.

'Hello,' he said, 'I thought you were never coming.'

'Well, that's a nice welcome, after I went to London to do your shopping,' she said, her voice soft and tender, showing a little of her joy in seeing him again.

'You got my toothpaste? All the way to London for that?' His voice was softer now and he smiled. 'You had a good time? Did Sister Odinga enjoy her steak?'

'How did you know she ate steak?'

'She does,' he said. 'I never forget what to order for my lady friends.'

'She said thank you and she would like to see you when you feel like it.'

He nodded. 'Soon.' It was the answer he gave to everyone who enquired. 'Who was that woman with the squeaky voice you left with me, yesterday?'

'She's very efficient,' said Nuala, her eyes dancing. He'd missed her and found her indispensable. It was wonderful. 'I have your other shopping here.' She brought the packages to the bedside for him to feel and handed him the change from the purchases. 'The scent is lovely,' she said. 'But perfume is a very individual choice. I like this one very much, but some people like more musky ones.' She was thinking of Trudie l'Estrade and wondering what she would say if given flowery perfume.

'It doesn't matter what the wearer likes. If I give

scent, it has to be to my taste. I'm the one to smell it.'

She chuckled. 'That's a novel way of looking at it. I know that the wearer hardly smells it at all after a few minutes, so it is worn for others to enjoy.'

'You seem pleased with yourself,' he said. I suppose that boyfriend swept you off your feet and you named the day.' His mouth was mocking again. 'What it is to be young and in love.'

'I'm twenty-two,' she said, with dignity. 'That's not young.'

'A child,' he said. 'You make me feel like Methusalah.'

'Age doesn't matter when one loves,' she said, greatly daring. 'You must know that.'

He stiffened and then smiled, ruefully. 'Love comes in many forms. I know about love.'

She busied herself with the wash basin and drink tray. Poor dear man. He was in love with Trudie and must be agonised at the thought of losing her if he could no longer take part in the wide range of activities that needed sight and co-ordination. Never to look at the woman he loved, never to see her expressions, never to know if she felt real love for him or if he was being pitied. The breakfast tray arrived and she sat near the bed to help him. It was a time that she enjoyed. He was close to her, dependent in a way and usually good-tempered after that first morning when he had yet to accept her help, but today her presence seemed to make him edgy.

Nuala couldn't understand it. She had fresh uniform on and the soap and talc she used were only slightly scented with an elusive flower perfume, so she knew that she couldn't offend in any way. The nurse who had taken her place must have ruffled him more than she knew.

'Come on, now, you must eat a little more. Would you like me to peel an orange or an apple? There's more fresh fruit for you.'

'I don't want it, damn you! I want to get up and feed myself. Can't you see, woman? I'm lying here with my manhood sapping from me while you peel me oranges.' He flung an arm across the table, sending the coffee pot flying. Hot liquid flowed over the two rugs covering the polished floor and Nuala gave a cry of pain as the scalding liquid touched her hand. 'What's happening? You're hurt. Nuala where are you? If you're scalded put it under the cold tap and keep it there until I tell you to stop.'

She ran the tap and looked back at the mess on the floor. 'It's all right. It was only a splash and it isn't going to blister. It was on the back of my left hand, and I was more startled than hurt.'

'Thank God. I'm sorry,' he said. 'I'm really sorry. I'm a little tense today. I'm having a visitor this afternoon.'

'Miss l'Estrade?'

'Yes, Trudie rang last night and said she would be in England for a week. She's coming here.'

Nuala forgot the spilled coffee and the slight pain in her hand. She went to the bedside and took his hand in both her small ones. 'You mustn't let it worry you. If she loves you, it will make no difference to her, whatever happens to you.'

'You think not?' She shook her head and then realised that he couldn't see her.

'What woman would want a man robbed of sight and incapable of doing the work for which he is fitted?'

'Any woman in love,' she said.

'And you, little nurse with the small hands and steely heart? Would you stay with a man for ever?'

'I would love him always,' she said, the tears starting. 'I am sure that she will love you as you want to be loved.'

He took her face in his hands and kissed her damp cheek. 'Such a fierce little champion,' he said. 'And yet you weep for me.' She drew back, ashamed that he should know of her tears.

'I must get something to clear up the mess,' she said, and fled from the room.

'Nurse Kavanagh. Whatever is the matter?'

'Mr Wendover knocked over the coffee. He was upset because his lady friend is coming to see him and he hates looking as he is.'

'And he took it out on you? I thought better of him, Nurse, but surely you know better than to shed tears over a bad-tempered patient?'

'Yes, Sister,' said Nuala. 'I have to wipe up the mess, Sister. The rugs are badly stained. Shall I bring them into the sluice room?'

'Do that, Nurse. We have this trouble at times, but pretty rugs make a room look more comfortable and cut down noise. They'll have to go for cleaning and I'll requisition two more from stores. We keep a few in reserve. Ask Annie to bring the polisher. He'll have to put up with a polished floor and no rugs until the fresh ones arrive.'

The ward maid buffed the floor and soon it shone again, reflecting the light from the windows. Nuala washed the bed table and polished it and the room smelled fresh and sweet. Blake Wendover seemed to have recovered and he talked about Switzerland, asking if Nuala had visited that country. She told him of her travels to France with nurses during her training, but admitted that as she had lovely places and the sea almost on the doorstep at home, she felt no need to travel far.

'Tell me who sent the flowers, today,' he said. She read the labels and then blushed. 'You hesitate and I suspect that you are blushing.'

'Why should I? It just seemed stupid. Yesterday it seemed a good idea for Odinga and me to send you some flowers, but you have so many.'

'I am flattered, but I shall be very annoyed if you have spent good money on me.' His voice sounded lighter, almost boyish. 'What are they? Bring them over here.'

'Very little,' said Nuala. 'A woman in Piccadilly was selling fresh primroses. I kept them cool last night and they are rather sweet.'

He held the small pot and inhaled the scent. 'They smell like you,' he said. 'Put them on the locker with the violets.'

'Would you like more coffee?' she asked, trying to hide her pleasure. 'That's if we can manage without spilling it?'

'I'll be very careful,' he said. 'After coffee, I'd better change my pyjamas. I think I spilled something on these.' She could see no stains, but knew that he wanted to look as smart as possible for the woman he loved. Nuala selected some pyjamas in dark red silk and he insisted that he was able to change without her help. Why does he need me if he doesn't let me help him? she thought, as she took the coffee cup back to the wing kitchen.

Lunch was over and the room looked elegant with masses of flowers and the brightly-polished floor. Nuala was uneasy. She wanted to catch a glimpse of Trudie l'Estrade, but she dared not stay when she was off duty and she had to make an appointment for her hair and meet Dermot again before he left for Ireland.

The sun shone and there was no sign of rain, so she slipped into a pair of thick cord jeans with a shirt of pale blue covered by a warm light mohair sweater of heather tones that was comfortable but made her look colourless. Dermot was waiting when she left the hairdressers after making an appointment for the following day and they strolled down to the tow path along the banks of the river and on to the canal bridge to the old town. There was a tea room, reminiscent of the one kept by an old lady in the village at home, a great success with American and French visitors who enjoyed trying English afternoon tea. Dermot ordered scones and jam and cream cakes and watched while Nuala poured tea from a curly-handled china tea pot into delicate cups.

'I hope your business meetings were a success,' she said.

'Fine, just fine,' he said. 'And how is your VIP patient?' His eyes were wary. 'You spend all day with just the one man. Is that usual?'

'He can't see until he has the eye operation,' she said. 'And he seems to like the way I do things.'

'You have a soft voice, Nuala. Anyone not see-

ing you would think you a very seductive beauty.'
There was irony in his voice.

'What rubbish.' She was annoyed. 'You said
there was nothing seductive about me. So how
could a man without sight get any such idea? Be-
sides, he is in love with a beautiful French-Swiss girl
who is probably with him now.'

'Is that so?' Dermot took another scone and
smiled. 'Love is in the air. It must be the spring.
When can we name the day, darling, because I am
not taking no for an answer.'

'But I told you that I was busy and have no such
plans, with you or anyone, Dermot.'

He looked sulky for long enough for her to recall
such moods and to know that he hadn't really
changed for the better. Then he laughed.

'What is it?'

'It isn't like you to be coy, Nuala, but I like it.'

'I am not being coy.' She searched her mind for a
topic that would place them on firmer ground. 'I
haven't heard from my Mother for ages. How was
she when you left?'

He went red. 'She was fine. I'm sorry, Nuala, she
asked me to give you a package and I forgot.'

Once more, she had the odd sensation that Dermot was holding something back and wasn't being
honest.

'What is it?'

'A package.' He shrugged and fished in the deep
pocket of his raincoat. 'It was addressed to you at
home, but as I was coming to England, I said I'd
bring it in case it went astray.'

'And nearly forgot to give it to me,' she said,
dryly.

'Aren't you going to open it?'

She looked at the stiff brown envelope rounded with papers. 'It can't be anything important. It might be the details of a superannuation scheme that most of the nurses join. I can bear to wait before I open it.'

'I'm sure it isn't that,' he said, then blushed again. 'Are these cakes all right for you or shall I ask for another selection?' He was embarrassed, and Nuala stared at him.

'How do you know what it is? Have you opened it?' she said, lightly. To her consternation he went an even deeper red.

'Of course not,' he said, furiously. 'Your mother hinted that it was some legal document.'

'Oh, I see,' she said, only half believing him. 'I'll still leave it for now.' She put it away safely in her bag and they finished tea. Dermot seemed to have recovered. 'I enjoyed my tea,' she said with truth. 'I wonder if Odinga would like some cakes?' She went to the shop counter where cakes sold in the café could also be bought and the assistant filled a cardboard box with a luscious selection of cream cakes. Dermot said goodbye, obviously trying to impress her with his new-found devotion and Nuala was completely unmoved. It was with relief that she saw him leave, knowing that she wouldn't see him for many weeks. How I've changed, she thought.

She changed back into uniform and wondered if she need work in Mr Wendover's room now that his loved one was with him. It could be awkward and she decided to speak to Sister French about it. She carried the box of cakes with her but found that

Odinga was off duty, so they had to go into the fridge until later.

Nuala braced herself and tapped on the door of the private room. Sister French was off duty and there was nobody who could tell her to go to another part of the wing to help, so she had to report back for at least a few minutes to see that all was well with her patient.

'Come in.' His voice was low and she discerned a trace of irritation. She sighed and went in. He must resent any intrusion if he had a limited time with Trudie.

'Ah, Nurse Kavanagh, I'd like you to meet Miss l'Estrade.'

Nuala stood half way between the bed and the door. As usual, her feet had made hardly a sound even now that the floor was free of rugs, and he had known it was her before she had a chance to speak.

'Trudie, this is the nurse who has cared for me since the accident.'

'How do you do,' Nuala said, shyly. Her colour was rising and she could do nothing about it. Trudie l'Estrade stared at her as if she wanted to remember every detail of the pale girl with freckles and fine uncontrolled hair, slender body and lack of presence. What she saw seemed to please her and she smiled. The man on the bed listened intently.

'This is a pleasure,' said Trudie l'Estrade. She gave a high, tinkling laugh that must have had its origins in the tenor cow bells of Switzerland. 'I wondered very much what the girl looking after my darling Blake would be like.' Her eyes flickered over the girl again, dismissing her as less than a threat and therefore fit for the work she had to do;

all the menial tasks that a man would never want done by a woman for whom he had any sexual feeling.

Nuala didn't need to stare. Her first glance was photographic, making a still picture of the only woman to break through the barrier that Blake Wendover had imposed between his sick-room and the outside world. She had come as if by right and now sat on the end of the bed, crushing the notice that told people to approach on that side only. For her, there could be no rules, no restrictions. The soft leather shoes made by the designer who supplied royal households, film stars and socialites, were cerise, and the sheer stockings of pale pink were echoed in the superbly-tailored suit of heavy silk. Trudie obviously knew that her legs were good and well-shaped as she extended one foot, arching her instep and showing the hint of a fine lace-edged under-skirt. From a trim waist, her bosom swelled luxuriantly under the patterned shirt, and on a chair, she had carelessly dropped a blonde mink jacket and a silk scarf.

'I'd like some tea, Blake,' she said. Nuala moved uneasily. It wasn't quite the time for the evening meal and there would be nobody in the diet kitchen prepared to make tea. Pots of tea were possible at any time of the day for patients and guests, accompanied by biscuits, but Nuala had a feeling that Miss l'Estrade was not going to be content with that.

'I can make some tea in the wing kitchen,' said Nuala, glad of an excuse to escape. The visitor seemed to take over the room, with her silken clothes, fine accessories and her heavy perfume.

The flowers banked on the sills and tables lost the battle as Trudie waved a small square of Brussells lace drenched in musky scent two feet away from the captive in bed.

'I'm hungry,' said Trudie, firmly. 'Send down to the kitchens and ask for cakes. I shall be satisfied with cakes if they are very good. You have cakes as we have them at home?' The sneer was slight but definite. Nuala glanced at the set face on the white pillow and couldn't bear to let a woman like Trudie l'Estrade think that his hospital was lacking in any way.

'I think it can be arranged,' said Nuala, softly. What a good thing it was that Nancy Odinga had been off duty and the cream cakes were still cool and fresh in the fridge. Blake Wendover turned towards her voice. 'I brought some very good cakes back with me,' said Nuala, and she wondered if there was a tiny smile trying to escape the line of his tense mouth.

Trudie stood up and paced the room, looking first at the flowers and then out of the windows. As Nuala left the room, she saw the marks on the surface of the parquet where the slender but sharp heels of the fashion shoes had bitten deeply into the polish. She must have paced the room a great deal since her arrival. The clatter of the heels was clear and crisp and Nuala hoped that Blake was unaware of the sound. She found a kettle that was almost boiling and turned up the heat. The cakes were very attractive and Nuala arranged them carefully on a rather pretty plate that had been left by a visitor who brought tempting snacks in for her husband regularly.

She cut thin bread and butter and found some raspberry preserve intended for Sister French. Recklessly, she opened a packet of chocolate biscuits that should have been shared among the staff, a present from a grateful patient, and loaded the tray.

As soon as she entered the room, she saw the frown on the lovely face and knew that Trudie had hoped to find fault with her meal. 'I didn't know that you had such cakes in hospital,' she said, and her voice was rather shrill.

'We get them from a special shop in the town,' said Nuala, sweetly. 'Which is your favourite, Mr Wendover? The chocolate box, the eclair or the pastries?'

His lips twitched but he said, solemnly, 'I'll have the eclair, if I may. I think you'll find these equal to any you have in Geneva, Trudie.'

'I'll leave you to pour tea,' said Nuala. There had even been a slice of lemon left from the pancakes someone had eaten for lunch, so Trudie had a choice of lemon or milk. 'I'll take the fresh batch of flowers into the other room and arrange them for the junior. I think they can do with a little help. If you need anything, please ring.'

CHAPTER SIX

THE daffodils receded into a blur as her eyes filled with tears. Nuala thrust a twig of palm in to form a backing to the tulips and picked up the cut ends of the flowers she had arranged so carefully. I shall have to go back in there soon, she thought. The expression on the face of the woman visiting Blake Wendover had left her in no doubt—she had been dismissed as a tiny little servant-type who could be made to fetch and carry and wait on the more affluent and influential, and Trudie had hoped to find fault with her, showing Blake Wendover firmly that she was in charge.

Nuala brushed away the tears. She hates me, now. She knows that I made every effort to prove her wrong and suspects that I have my own pride, too. I wonder what they are saying about me now they are alone again? She regretted her gesture of independence. It would have been more diplomatic to have made tea and received the pitying conde-scension of the beautiful woman than to have made her angry. The enormous blue eyes had narrowed as she watched Nuala leave, and they held sus-picion and malice, as if she was wondering what went on in that untidy little head.

The sound of a door opening and a woman's voice made Nuala start and hastily wrap up the rubbish before throwing it in the bin. It was a high-pitched voice and easily recognisable. The

111

tap, tap of high heels on the tiled corridor could only be her urgent steps. Nuala stayed behind the closed door until the footsteps died away in the direction of the lift, then she peeped out, saw that Trudie had really gone and went back to the flower trolley belonging to the semi-private ward. She had arranged only one vase when a bell rang and she saw that the light had gone on over the door of her charge. The bell continued to ring, furiously.

He was sitting back on the pillows with a face like a thundercloud. 'Where have you been?' he said.

'I asked you to ring if you needed me,' she said.

'Well, I rang.'

'And I came at once, Mr Wendover.' It was too bad. Whatever had made him angry could have nothing to do with her. 'Are you uncomfortable? Shall I make your bed again?'

'No, leave it. It's full of crumbs, but it can wait.'

'It won't take a minute. If you move over to the edge, I can brush them out this side and then do the other.'

'Leave it, I said. Where did you get those cakes?'

'The cakes?' She tried to laugh. 'I bought them to eat with Nancy Odinga. I found that she was off duty, so they were sitting in the fridge until I went off duty. What a good thing I had them here.' He scowled. 'Well, you wouldn't want Miss L'Estrade to think we couldn't supply all you need for your guests, would you?' A faint smile began and she took courage. 'I hope you enjoyed them and that Miss l'Estrade made a good tea?'

'She nearly drowned me. Why didn't you stay to help me?' So that was the reason for his bad temper.

'Oh, I'm very sorry. I thought that you would like to be alone. I should have known that you wouldn't want Miss l'Estrade to feed you.'

'Why not?'

'Well, it often embarrasses people to have their loved ones wait on them, and I should have stayed.'

'Some people may think like that, but others have to endure it,' he said. She sighed. 'All right, you did what you thought was right for me. I'm sorry if I barked at you, but I found this afternoon rather trying.'

'Of course you did,' she said in a soothing tone. 'It must have been an ordeal, but I assure you that you don't look like a fragile patient, if that's the impression you thought you might give. You look very normal, except for the bandage, and I'm sure that it would make no difference to her even if you looked ill.'

'Trudie hates sickness. She is as healthy as a carthorse.'

'Hardly the nicest term to use about such a lovely lady,' she said, trying to sound disapproving.'

'She is rather beautiful. What was she wearing?'

Nuala described her in great detail, her heart nearly breaking. As she talked, the picture emerged of a lovely woman with every advantage and a dynamic personality.

'Yes, she has a lot of life,' said Mr Wendover when she stopped. 'That was a very generous description you gave, Nuala.' He grinned. 'A little more generous than the one she gave of you.'

'I expect she was right,' said Nuala, with the composure of despair. She could imagine Trudie almost licking her lips over the telling. She wouldn't spare a single detail if it was to convince her man that the soft-spoken nurse was ugly. 'I'm not much to write home about.'

'That's the impression she tried to give me. Tell me, Nuala, are you the only woman who can be objective in your praise of another woman?' She was surprised and rather touched. 'I can imagine everything you said about Trudie, but I can't believe that what she said about you is right.'

'What did she say?'

'I'm not telling. I have my own opinion of you and when these damned pads are gone, I shall judge for myself. Now, I think it's time for dinner. I heard the lift go some time ago.'

'Is Miss l'Estrade coming back tonight?'

'No. I sent her off to have dinner with a colleague of mine who rang up when you were out. She can spend the evening charming him. He's very susceptible to blondes.'

'I thought you could have eaten together. I ordered an extra dinner for her if she wanted to stay.'

'Determined to keep her in this room with me?'

'I was only trying to make it easy for you to enjoy her company while she is here.'

'Even though you can't stand her?'

'That isn't fair. I have said nothing to justify such a remark.'

'I apologise. It's just that she is such a different type from you. I couldn't imagine either of you wanting the other's company for more than half an hour at a time.' Less than that, thought Nuala. 'She is staying in London for a few days but will call in here tomorrow before she leaves. I asked my secretary to write a letter for me which Trudie will take and deliver when she returns to France.'

'I thought you were planning to see her in Geneva? Does she live in France?'

'I had a congress lined up in Geneva about the trends in micro-surgery and she would have been there with her brother. That's the surgeon to whom I'm writing. He's a brilliant man in his field and I want details about the conclusions reached.' She was silent. 'You disapprove of my dictating to my secretary over the phone? Heavens, girl, I have to do something or I'll go mad.'

'Is Miss l'Estrade a surgeon?'

He laughed. 'Not likely. She hates illness and I could tell how restless she was in here. I hope the floor can be repolished. She must have left tram-lines over it.'

'It's difficult to keep quiet on parquet,' said Nuala.

'What are you writing?'

'What sharp ears. I'm making a new notice to pin on the bed. I'm afraid your guest sat on the other one.'

'I tried to tell her that it wasn't allowed, but she only laughed. It was like sitting in a storm-tossed boat, with her wriggling about on the end of the bed.'

Nuala regarded him, solemnly. He wasn't joking. 'I'll get your dinner,' she said, and pinned the new notice to the end of the bed cover, smoothing away the creases as best she could.

'Before you go, open a window.'

'It's cold outside. Would the door do?'

'No, I'll keep well down under the clothes, but I

can't eat with that heavy scent about the room. It's terrible.'

'Did you give her the new scent? If she thinks you prefer lighter perfumes, she will take the hint, I expect.'

The evening air came in cool and fresh and they could hear a bird singing on its way to roost. The air cleared and Nuala shut the window again, drew the curtains and went to fetch the tray. She noticed that Blake Wendover hadn't actually said if Trudie liked her present or not. Perhaps she had stuffed it into her bag, unopened. Which would she be wearing on her next visit?

Blake Wendover settled down, enjoyed his meal and told Nuala about the congress in Geneva. He made her laugh as he described some of the misunderstandings between men and women from different countries, confronted with other languages, and went on to say how he loved waterskiing. She wondered how he could bear to talk about the sports he might never enjoy again and admired his resilience. Now that Trudie was out of the building, he seemed more relaxed and they shared the intimacy of the warm quiet room while she read to him again from the book of poems. Sister French came back on duty and wanted to know who had brought in the cream cakes left over in the fridge.

'Nurse Kavanagh bought them, knowing that I had a French-Swiss guest who enjoys such gooey confections.' His voice was bland, as if Nurse Kavanagh had bought them at his bidding. 'Please eat the rest, Sister,' he said, airily. 'Nurse will buy me some more tomorrow, if I ask nicely.'

It was his way of saying that he would replace them and Nuala warmed to his tact. 'They were fresh today, Sister. If you take them, I shall have no fear that my patient, who also seemed to enjoy gooey cakes, will put on weight.'

He put his hands behind his head and the long line of his spare body was firm under the covers. 'If I put on weight, you'll have to race round the park with me, Nurse Kavanagh.' Her heart lurched. Was he hinting that when he was discharged from hospital, possibly blind, he wanted her to go with him and be his guide and nurse?

'We have the reports from your two surgeons, Mr Wendover,' said Sister French. Nuala wanted to hold his hand as the knuckles showed white with tension.

'And?' he said, sharply.

'They say that there is an area of detachment which they want to treat.' Sister French looked as if she wished she could have handed her unpleasant task to the surgeons who had made the decision, but she went on. 'The condition has improved with bed rest, but it has reached its limit of recovery without surgery.'

'Thank you, Sister. I know from experience how trying it is to pass on such news. Well,' he said, exhaling slowly, 'the sooner the better.'

'I'll be in touch with Mr Micheljon. He said he'll see you the day after tomorrow to finalise arrangements.' Nuala clenched her hands, knowing how he must be suffering. Sister French lingered for a few minutes, asking if she could send a secretary for him to dictate letters, but he shook his head. 'I'll say goodnight,' she murmured, glad to leave them.

'At least you'll have Miss l'Estrade with you for a while. I expect she'll be able to put back her return to France if you want her to stay,' said Nuala.

'I expect she would, but I shan't ask her,' he said. 'I'd rather you made no mention of this to her when she comes again.'

'But she will want to know. Surely she has a right to be at your side when you are recovering from surgery?' If you were mine, her heart cried, I would be with you day and night and never leave your side.

'She doesn't like sickness,' he repeated. 'Say nothing to her,' he commanded. 'I shall hope to leave it until she goes away. It can wait for a day or so. I'll try to arrange it for the seventeenth.'

'St Patrick's Day,' she said. 'I had forgotten until now. Maybe it will be lucky for you.'

'If he's your saint, how can it fail?' His mouth was sad.

'I have shamrock sent to me every year. I hope they remember it. It might have come already,' she said.

'Shamrock . . . the wearing of the green,' he lay back and smiled. 'I can imagine you wearing it.'

'You have no idea how I look with or without shamrock,' she said.

'You forget that Trudie described you,' he teased, and she was glad to see him smile.

'I'm going shopping tomorrow in the main part of town. Is there anything you want? I'd better get some biscuits to replace the ones I used from the wing kitchen and you need more tissues.' She added several items to her list and slipped it into the pocket of her dress. It was long after her time for leaving the wing, and she had no further excuse for staying. He seemed sleepy as she opened the door to go.

'Don't forget,' he said. 'You say nothing to Trudie.'

Nuala walked back to her bedroom. He must love Trudie l'Estrade very much to want her shielded from pain and the anxiety of knowing how he was suffering. She wondered bitterly if Trudie l'Estrade knew what a wonderful man loved her. She doubted if she was worthy of that love. Nuala sighed. If she had needed anything to tell her that there was no chance of Blake Wendover ever caring for her, one glance at Trudie must be enough to quench even the hope of an enduring friendship with him. Who wants enduring friendship when a heart cries out for love?

The coat she had been wearing that afternoon was lying across the bed in her room and Nuala took it to hang in the wardrobe. Her handbag caught her attention and she recalled the package that Dermot had given her from her mother in Ireland. She had forgotten everything about her off duty, except for the buying of the cakes. She smiled. There was a tap on her door and she knew it might be Odinga. 'Sorry,' said Nuala. 'I bought some nice cakes for you but they got eaten by a glamorous Swiss woman.'

'Not to worry, I'm not hungry,' said Odinga, throwing her coat on the chair. 'Sorry if I came at a bad moment. You want to open your mail?'

'It's nothing. I met Dermot and this was from my mother. He nearly forgot to give it to me, but I happened to say I should have heard from her and he went red and brought it out of his pocket, with many apologies.'

'It looks official. I can never wait to open anything. It's more than a letter from home.'

'Dermot said he thought it was a document of some kind,' said Nuala, vaguely. 'It might be details of the nurses' superannuation scheme. I haven't had time to open it.' She looked at it without interest. 'He didn't think it was that,' she said, turning the envelope over. He had flushed when she joked about him opening it, but now she saw the thin line of fresh gum that re-sealed an opened letter. She picked up her letter knife and opened the package as if it contained a rattlesnake, and unfolded the documents. It was a letter from a solicitor and she sat on the bed to unravel the mystery while Odinga went down to fetch coffee.

She felt sick, knowing that Dermot had known all the time she was with him what the document contained. Her mind was a blank sheet of ice as she thought of the smooth-talking man who she had learned to know as the true Dermot, a man of low principles and avaricious mind. He had known, before she had the news, of her inheritance, her grandmother's house and a useful income that would make her a very acceptable bride. The will had been passed for probate and she could use the income at once.

So now I have another burden. I'm not pretty and I shall think that any man who shows the slightest interest in me is after the house and the money, she thought.

'Coffee?' Odinga brought in a tray. 'I'll go if you want to be alone,' she said.

'No, please hear the latest saga about my beautiful friend, Dermot.' She told her the details and
listened with some pleasure to the opinion that the
other girl had formed of the man.

'At least you can have a certain independence
and afford good holidays, but it was as well you
heard about this before you gave your word to
marry him. I think you were beginning to feel that
you had misjudged him.' Nuala nodded. 'Go down
and ring the pub where he's staying. Finish it
tonight and then you can forget him and remember
the goodness of your grandmother.'

As soon as the coffee was finished, Nuala went
down to the telephone and rang the pub number.
There were no specific arrangements to meet as
Dermot had some more business to attend to in
London, so Nuala didn't ask to speak to him. She
left a short message, that it would be impossible to
see him before he returned to Ireland. I couldn't
bear to hear his voice, she decided. She signed the
necessary papers and packed them ready to return
to the solicitor, putting them back into the fresh
cover provided and already stamped. They think of
everything, she thought, and slipped down to the
lodge so that it could catch the first post out in the
morning.

'Did you get your other package, Nurse?' The
porter smiled. 'I put it in the cool in the office as it
looked like flowers or plants.'

She thanked the night porter and took the damp
bundle to her room. Her eyes softened. Her aunt
had remembered to send her some shamrock. She
took a tiny spray and held it to her cheek. It was
cool and fresh and very green and smelled of the

fields of home. Tears of loneliness threatened, but she busied herself, tying it into tiny bunches ready to give to her friends on St Patrick's Day. They would keep in the cool box in the fridge for as long as she wanted them.

She wondered what St Patrick would have for her in future years. If Blake Wendover had his operation on that day, it would colour the memory each time it came round. If he lost his sight, she would weep for him each time she saw the green leaves. There was so little time now before a decision had to be made and once Mr Micheljon made up his mind about a case, it was as good as done. Her hands were cold with fear as she slipped into a hot bath and tried to relax. If she could be with him in the theatre, she could send out waves of her love to help him. Such feelings must have their use, even if they could have no influence on the surgeon's skill. It was a stupid idea, but she prayed for him and willed him to get better.

Heavy-eyed, Nuala woke and wondered why she was so depressed. She washed her swollen face and applied more make-up than usual, reminding herself that she must be calm if he wasn't to detect something in her voice that would give away the secret that she was in love with him.

The night staff were still busy and Nuala wondered if an emergency had been admitted. Sister French was in her office and waited impatiently for Nuala to shut the door. 'There's been a change of plan,' she said. 'Last night Mr Wendover didn't sleep well and Mr Micheljon thinks that the sooner he operates, the sooner the tension will be over. I can't help linking the restlessness with the visit of his fiancée yesterday.' Sister French looked cross. 'I didn't want her to stay for so long, but she assured me that they are to be married shortly, and she had every right to be with him. What she didn't know was that his temperature shot up last night and he doesn't look very happy.'

'How is he now, Sister? Do I give him breakfast?'

'No, he's sleeping now. Mr Micheljon is getting his team assembled and in half an hour I'll give the pre-medication. As he hasn't eaten since last night, they can carry on as soon as they like.'

'I'll stay outside in case he rings, or would you rather I helped in semi-private?'

'No, I'd rather you were with him until he leaves for the theatre, Nurse, but as he's asleep and may be for an hour, would you pop over for my post and newspaper? I had no time to get them after receiving a call to come on duty early.'

Nuala hurried down to the lodge and collected the letters and papers, then glanced at her watch. She ran across to the flat and took the smaller plastic envelope into which she had put two bunches of shamrock the night before, tucking them into her pocket and making sure they weren't crushed. She rummaged for small safety pins and ran back to the wing. Sister French was in semi-private and just raised a hand in acknowledgement of her nurse's return before going back to her patient, and Nuala stole into the room where Blake Wendover lay.

The morning sun shone with a dull glint of gold, promising more brightness later, but Nuala couldn't bring herself to look at it. All this, and the coming spring might be gone for ever for this man if the operation was a failure. She sat quietly by the bed and watched him breathing. His mouth was relaxed and in sleep showed none of the frustration that had built up over the past week. She touched his hair where it showed above the neat bandage and took her hand away, sharply as he stirred. 'Nurse Nuala?' he said.

'Yes, I'm here.' He was drowsy or he wouldn't have smiled so tenderly. He would have smiled like that even if it had been Sister Frazer at his side, as he was slightly high on sleeping pills.

'Nurse Nuala,' he said again, as if the words amused him. He put out his hand and she put hers into it, after a moment of hesitation. He squeezed it firmly and she knew that he was fully awake. 'This is the day,' he said.

'Yes, Mr Micheljon is getting ready,' she said.

'Trudie isn't here?' The strong fingers dug into her wrist, hurting her. But it wasn't his fingers that bruised her heart. He cared so much for the beautiful blonde woman who had claimed to be engaged to him that he couldn't allow her to see his suffering, and wanted to shield her from anything unpleasant.

'No, they haven't told her yet.'

'Thank God for that,' he said. 'Promise me you will keep her away until I'm better? I want at least a full day before she can come to see me, even if she camps on the doorstep.'

'I'll do my best, but, as she told Sister French, she is engaged to you and has the right to come in to see you.'

'I say no!'

'All right, all right,' soothed Nuala. 'I'll let her in over my dead body,' she said. 'But you must lie still and think beautiful thoughts.' He sighed. 'I've brought you a present for good luck,' she said. He heard the faint rustling of the plastic and put out a hand. 'It isn't a cream cake,' she joked, her face stiff with sorrow. No man would ever feel as fiercely for her as this man did for Trudie l'Estrade. 'I've brought some shamrock and I'm going to pin it on your theatre gown. It won't show under the towels and it will be good for you to know . . .'

'To know what, Nuala?'

'Just that you have friends and staff who want you well again,' she said, in confusion.

He fingered the tiny bunch of green leaves, gently. 'Thank you. Are you wearing it too?'

'I shouldn't wear it today, but I will for you,' she said. 'I have mine pinned to my uniform.'

'Let me feel it. I must know that you are wearing it.' She took his hand and rested it on the spray on her bosom. He pressed gently and smiled, with a hint of his good humour. 'Not as Trudie said at all. You have the downy breast of a dove.' She stepped back, blushing. 'Forgive me,' he said. 'The drugs are making me stupid.'

Sister French came in with the pre-medication of Omnopon and Scopolamine and the two women changed his pyjamas for a theatre gown. Sister French teased him about the shamrock and said that all the staff should wear it to give him additional luck.

'I have more in my room, Sister,' said Nuala.

'Just give a sprig to Sister, Nurse Kavanagh,' said Blake Wendover. 'I don't want to push it too far.

But you must both promise me to wear it so that if I can see, I shall see the shamrock first.'

Nuala saw that Sister French was fighting her own tears and told him to try and sleep. 'I'll stay until the trolley comes, Sister.'

'Go to the theatre and hand him over to the anaesthetist personally, Nurse Kavanagh,' she said.

In a few minutes, the drug was taking a firm hold on his senses and Nuala knew that he had lost all sense of reality, but he clutched her hand as she walked by the side of the trolley all the way up to the theatre complex. It wasn't the grip of a man who knew nothing of his surroundings and she could sense the intense magnetism of the man through this slight contact, demanding a response from her. She squeezed his hand and then let it go as the theatre nurse came to take over.

Nuala went back to the room and stripped the bed, ready for making up with fresh linen and a cover as the pretty linen bedspread had suffered a maze of creases when Miss l'Estrade had sat on it. The junior nurse came to help and the bed was soon neatly made with the side folded back to receive the patient on his return. The flowers, as ever, were waiting to be arranged, and the junior was wheeling a trolley over to collect them when Nuala heard the tip-tap of high heels on the corridor floor.

'Where is he?' Trudie l'Estrade looked more annoyed than anxious.

'There was a sudden change of treatment,' said Nuala, politely.

'Why was I not told?'

The junior nurse watched, open-mouthed. Trudie was wearing a bright red cossack-style coat with black froggings and a hat of astrakan fur on her beautifully coiffured hair. Her soft leather boots were not high fashion, but whatever she wore became the right thing for her to wear and Nuala could imagine no fashion writer daring to find fault.

'There was no time. Visitors were not allowed this morning before Mr Wendover went to the theatre as he had drugs to relax him and prepare him for the operation.'

'I could have been told. I think perhaps you forgot to tell me.' She stared at Nuala with growing resentment. 'Of course, it might be that you didn't want me here with your Mr Wendover. I have heard of little nurses who fall in love with their pet patients, even if they have no hope of being loved.'

'That's not fair.' The junior nurse was pink-cheeked and indignant. 'If Nurse Kavanagh needs love, she can get it from her own boyfriend. He's the best looking man I've seen, off a cinema screen, for years.'

'Dermot?' It came without even thinking. 'Thank you, Nurse, but I'm sure that Miss l'Estrade isn't interested in my private affairs. I'm sure she must be worried and wants to know what is happening in the theatre.' Inwardly, Nuala blessed her nosy little junior nurse for staring at her when she was with Dermot in the hotel bar. At least he's been a help today, she thought.

'Oh, I see. Yes, I wish to know everything,' said Trudie, gathering her wits again. If it wasn't so insulting, it would be funny to be almost told that she could never attract a really good-looking man, and Trudie couldn't hide her surprise.

'I think you should see Sister French,' said Nuala. 'She will be in her office, if you would come this way.'

Sister French looked surprised to see her visitor. 'I asked Mr Wendover who I should telephone and he forbade me to contact anyone but his mother,' she said. 'She *is* his next of kin and he has no wife,' she added.

'But we are engaged,' said Trudie. Sister French glanced at her white hands and brightly-enamelled finger nails, noting the absence of rings. Trudie waved one hand, with studied nonchalance. 'It is not in the papers yet,' she said, 'but we have an understanding.'

'I'm afraid that in this hospital we contact only those who are on the list given us by the patient and the legal next-of-kin,' said Sister, politely. She smiled. 'But I know you must be worried about him. Please sit down and have coffee with me and I'll tell you all I can.' She looked at Nuala, who went to the kitchen to ask the nurse there to take an extra cup in when Sister had coffee, and then went back to the flowers.

'Is that shamrock you're wearing?' asked the junior nurse, enviously. 'You wouldn't have a sprig to spare, would you?'

Nuala remembered what had been said before Blake Wendover was taken to the theatre. He wanted only Sister and his own personal nurse to wear it until he came back to the wing. Nuala locked this privilege into her heart and decided that, this year, no other person should share her custom. 'I'm sorry, I gave a spare piece to Mr Wendover for luck,' she said. 'Next year, perhaps, if we're both here.'

'You'll be back home and married to that man you were with, Nurse.'

She was becoming too inquisitive and Nuala told her that she would finish the flowers if Nurse could report to the kitchen to give out morning drinks. Where shall I be next year? she thought when she was alone. Where would Blake Wendover be and what would life hold for him? She couldn't imagine Trudie as a patient wife taking a blind man on her travels or settling down with him, even in a country as lovely as Switzerland. She finished the flowers and looked back into the immaculate room before going to Sister to report off for the afternoon.

'I could wait to see Mr Wendover back in bed,' she said.

'He won't be coming back immediately, Nurse. Mr Micheljon wants him near the eye theatre so that he can assess him as soon as he is conscious. He might come back here with black-out glasses instead of that hot bandage. As the detached area is small and low down, they hope that gravity will assist the healing and he will be nursed sitting up and be able to sit out in a chair.'

'But that's wonderful, Sister.'

Sister French looked at the girl's shining eyes. 'He will be nursed like that whatever the outcome of the operation, Nurse. We don't know what the result will be. I want to thank you for all the quiet, personal touches you have added to his nursing, like this.' She touched the sprig of shamrock she wore. 'I know it means a lot to him as it would to any patient in that condition. Some men and women, carry the most absurd things to theatre with them, from old teddy bears to photographs of their children, and we allow it as they are in a weakened state and need these touches. I hope he sees it tomorrow.'

'If it is a success, will he be in total darkness again?'

'He might have a pinhole of light in the very middle of the lenses almost at once, so that he can see in one direction only. With recovery, the hole is widened. We do it with dense sticking plaster so that it can be peeled back in tiny sections. It works better than some more ponderous methods and the patient can wear glasses that fit.'

'Is there anything more I can do, Sister.'

Sister French glanced at her with sharp eyes. 'Yes, you can go off duty and do something specific. It's wrong to mope over a patient, as you know, and I can't have you losing weight over Blake Wendover.'

'I shan't do that, Sister.' Nuala blushed. 'I'll go to the library and fetch my clothes from the cleaners,' she said, convincingly.

'Is that a promise? Good, you can change my books, too,' said Sister French.

CHAPTER SEVEN

THE telephone was ringing in one of the rooms
when Nuala went back on duty. She rushed to
Blake's room thinking it could be the operator
calling her to take messages from outside, as no
direct calls were allowed in the room. She made a
mental note to unplug the set now that the room
was empty. Sister French or the wing secretary
could answer any enquiries while her patient was in
the eye theatre.

'Hello,' she said, breathlessly. 'This is Nurse
Kavanagh, private wing St Jude's.'

'Are you Blake's nurse? But of course you are.
He told me about your soft Irish voice and he was
right. I approve.'

'Who is this please?' Nuala had never heard the
voice but warmed to its owner at once.

'He's not there, is he?' the woman whispered.
'I'm a bit late ringing and he likes me to ring when
you are off duty,' she said, cheerfully. 'Oh, by the
way, I'm his mother. He says you bully him, but
you don't sound like an Amazon.'

'Mrs Wendover? Has Sister French contacted
you?'

'You mean about his operation?' The voice was
low, and Nuala could sense the undercurrent of
anxiety. 'It's tomorrow, isn't it? I wanted to wish
him luck.'

131

'Oh, dear, you haven't heard the latest message?'

'I've been away from my flat for two days. Is anything wrong?'

'No, everything is fine, but they decided to operate today as there was no point in waiting.'

'Oh, why wasn't I by the phone? I expect they tried to reach me. To tell you the truth, I couldn't stand having Trudie l'Estrade telling me what I ought to do with my life. She wanted to stay with me for a day or so, but I said I had to go away. Has she been to the hospital?'

'Yes, she came twice.'

'That's enough to send up his pulse rate,' Mrs Wendover said, dryly. 'Not the most restful sick visitor.'

Nuala warmed even more to the mother of Blake Wendover. 'I'll ask Sister if there's any news from the theatre,' she said, and ran to the office to bring Sister French to the telephone.

'I'm Sister French. Your son is now in recovery and Mr Micheljon is hoping to send him back to us tomorrow about lunch time. He has made a good recovery from anaesthetic and his general condition is excellent.' She listened. 'I promise to ring as soon as I hear any more news, and please feel free to contact me again. At worst, he will be as he was yesterday, but Mr Micheljon is the best in his field and an authority on laser work.' She listened again. 'Yes, he will be able to come home soon. There will be no further surgical treatment.'

Sister saw Nuala standing by her side, listening. She handed the receiver to the girl, saying that Mrs Wendover wanted to speak to her again. 'Come to my office when you are free,' she added.

'Nurse Kavanagh. If my son is blind, will you come and stay with me for a few days to tell me what to do?' There was desperation in the voice and Nuala shared the other woman's sorrow.

'I'd do all I could to help in any way,' she said, 'But isn't there someone who would want to be with him?'

'I'm all he has,' said his mother, simply.

'I mean Miss l'Estrade, his fiancée.'

'His *what*? Oh, no, don't tell me that she finally caught him? I've been praying that she would never marry him, but I know how attractive she can be when she puts her mind to it.' She controlled her voice. 'I don't care. I shall insist that he comes to me until he has convalesced, and for that, I shall need help from someone skilled, like you.'

'Don't you think we ought to wait and see what Mr Wendover has to say about it?'

His mother chuckled. 'Oh, you have got to know him well. He can be very stubborn if he can't have what he wants. Is he a terrible patient?'

'Terrible, but I manage,' said Nuala.

'Could I ring you later?'

'Of course. Sister said that you must telephone at any time.'

'I don't mean that. I want to speak to you, personally. Is that allowed?'

'I'm sure that Sister wouldn't object. You have this number, but I can give you the number of the place where I live. It's next door to the hospital and someone can leave a message if I'm not there and I could ring back, if that would help?'

'Oh, it would. Bless you, for that.'

Nuala took down the telephone number of Mrs Wendover's flat and gave her the one of the nurses' hostel. As she went to the office, she had a strong feeling that, given the chance, she could be good friends with the older woman. He calls her Mattie, she recalled. It suits her.

Sister French put down the house phone and looked up, smiling.

'You wanted me, Sister?'

'Yes, Nurse Kavanagh.'

'I usually come back to make Mr Wendover comfortable, but as he isn't here and the room is tidy, I could help out in the other rooms before I go to supper.'

'Thank you, Nurse, but we aren't very busy tonight. You've worked hard and stayed on duty for longer than was fair.' Nuala blushed, with a slightly guilty feeling that Sister took it for granted that her devotion to duty was the sole reason for staying, taking care of her patient long after she could have left him at night. 'I think you could go off duty after supper and just run a few errands before it's time to go down.'

'Thank you, Sister.' Nuala stood by the desk, waiting for her instructions.

'I also wanted to say how much I like your new appearance, Nurse. It suits you and makes you much tidier.' Sister smiled. The soft hairstyle and discreet make-up gave the impression of a sweet-faced girl with gentle eyes. Instead of looking boyish, the heart-shaped face and the now muted freckles, gave a sweet air of femininity.

'Thank you,' said Nuala, recalling that Sister was the third person to remark on her new look. She was conscious of added confidence when she saw her own reflection and her duty cap was much easier to wear. 'What errands have you for me, Sister?'

'Just take some things up to recovery for Mr Wendover. His toilet bag and a pair of fresh pyjamas should be enough until he returns tomorrow. I doubt if you will see him and he must not be disturbed, even by other staff, but you could peep in. Leave the case on the table for the nurse on duty to deal with if she isn't in the room at the time.'

'I'll go now, Sister, but what do I do tomorrow?'

'Would you take the morning off and do a shift from two onwards? That should cover the time when he comes back and you will be here to settle him for the night.' She sighed. 'I hate messing up off duty, but sometimes I have no alternative.'

'I don't mind,' said Nuala, with a bright smile. *Not mind?* It was the understatement of the year. She was delighted to think that once back in the wing, he would again be in her care. She packed the small case and took it to the lift and up to the next floor where the smaller theatre units existed with a six-bedded room for recovery. Each bed was cubicled with curtains that could be swished back as soon as the patient was over the immediate post-operative stage. There was no staff in the outer office and a light showing in the eye theatre told of nurses busily clearing up after a list.

Two of the cubicles were tightly curtained, but the one by the desk had a gap between the drapes. Nuala peeped in and saw Blake Wendover propped up in bed, appearing quite normal. He sat upright, a very good looking man, wearing sunglasses, or so it would seem to the casual observer. His hair was brushed and his face had a healthy glow, showing that only a light anaesthetic had been given, to make sure that he suffered no attacks of vomiting after the operation and so put no strain on the newly treated tissues.

At a loss because there seemed to be no suitable place where she could leave the clothes outside the cubicle, Nuala parted the curtains more and quietly put the case at the foot of the bed on the floor, where it would be easily seen by whoever came near the bed. She straightened and looked at the man on the bed. The dark glasses stared at her and, for a moment, she thought that he must be able to see her, but he merely said, 'If that's my case, just leave it and I'll tell the nurse when she comes back.'

She backed away without speaking, having been forbidden to talk to him and knowing that once she spoke, she would have to stay and tell him about the call from his mother and about Miss l'Estrade's visit that morning. Her eyes were misty as she watched him for a full minute, her hand touching the tiny wilting sprig of shamrock on her breast. She could have wept openly when she saw that the sprig she had given him was in water by the bed. I hope it brought you luck, she thought as she went slowly down the stairs and out into the corridor leading to the cafeteria.

'Coming to the concert this evening?' said Junior Sister Maggie Rich. 'Haven't seen you for ages in the sitting-room.'

'I've been specialling until late at night,' said Nuala.

'Nice work if you can get it,' said Maggie, cheerfully. 'We've been very busy.'

'I know,' said Nuala, wanting to ask the one question in her mind and knowing that she couldn't talk shop about one of the consultants in the open cafeteria. 'I might come,' she said, not being able to think of an excuse to stay away from the social activities of the staff. I can't say I'm going to wash my hair. That would seem like a rebuff, and I do want to get to know some of the other nurses. I can't let the memory of one man in dark glasses dominate my thoughts and my future, when I know that I can never share that future with him.

'I'll call for you when I come off duty,' said Maggie. 'We're nearly straight and I have only a few drums to supervise and send for autoclaving. I want to catch up with all your news.'

Nuala finished her meal and decided to make coffee to drink in the common room in the hostel while she waited for Maggie. She welcomed the invitation and hoped that she could find out a little about the condition of her patient beyond the cautious hospital hand-out bulletin of 'he's as well as can be expected'.

Sister Odinga came in, sniffing the air. 'I thought it was proper coffee,' she said. 'I came over with a book I borrowed from Rich, but I wouldn't say no to a cup of that coffee.'

'You're welcome,' said Nuala.

'How's your patient? I hear it was done today.'

'He's in recovery, but that's all I do know. I saw him for a second when I took some clean clothes up to the unit, but I was forbidden to speak to him. He looked very well,' she said. 'I wish I could find out more, but I suppose they will be cautious in letting any news go out that might upset his mother.'

'Or that lovely creature who comes to see him. When is that trendy fiancée coming to scoop him up?'

'His mother has other ideas,' said Nuala with a smile. 'She sounds a lovely lady.'

'And you agree with her, by the sound of it,' said Odinga, shrewdly. She noted the slight blush that tinged the delicate cheeks, but said nothing. 'You were going to tell me more about your legacy.'

'Yes.' The girl's relief was obvious at the change in the conversation. 'It consists mostly of a rather nice big old house by the water in a small town in Ireland. My grandmother, and my aunt who lived with her for years, used to look after me for weeks in the holidays, so I suppose they got quite fond of me.' She sighed. 'It's a wonderful feeling, knowing that she loved me enough to want to give me independence, but in a way, it ties me to one of two decisions.'

'I wouldn't quarrel with a gift like that.'

'I don't. I would love to keep it as a holiday home, but it would be wicked to leave it empty for most of the year. Even if I let it out, I couldn't cope with it from this side of the Irish sea. I have to live there or sell it. I haven't enough money to put a housekeeper there to look after my interests while I'm working here.'

'What is it suitable for?'

'It would make a good convalescent home or a small hotel.' She stared at the darkened window. 'It would make a perfect holiday home. I'd like that, and to be able to invite my friends there. I know several people who have very little money who would be thrilled to be invited to a place like that for a week or so. The money that goes with the legacy isn't sufficient for that, so I shall have to make up my mind to lose it and build up capital for my old age,' she said, trying to speak of it lightly.

Maggie joined them and looked with approval at Nuala. 'You look so much better than when you came. I know you've had a hair-do, but your clothes seem prettier and . . . everything.'

Nuala smoothed down the sleek velvet jeans that she had once put in the back of her cupboard as unsuitable to wear, and wondered why they now felt right with the pretty mohair sweater she had received for her birthday from her more adventurous cousin. They finished the coffee and went across to the main building to the concert in the medical school. Nuala sank into a deep armchair and gave up her mind to the flowing music of Brahms and Chopin. I'm glad I came, she thought. The music filled her heart with soft languor and she wondered if Blake Wendover liked music.

It was cheering to be greeted warmly by the other nurses and sisters, and one of the registrars who wandered in half way through the concert recognised her from her training days and sat with her talking during the interval. He asked what her plans might be, apart from the temporary job she had as relief nurse.

Maggie Rich laughed. 'A little bird told me that Nuala has a very dishy Irish boyfriend who wants to marry her,' she said.

Nuala blushed, with annoyance and not with the confusion of a girl in love, but she made no effort to deny the statement. After all, Dermot had asked her to marry him, and he was dishy if one liked the sensuality of his mouth and the impatience of his nature.

If the rumours spread and Mr Wendover heard them, it might be as well. It would then be easy to convince him that her loving care was routine for every patient and that her heart was lost elsewhere. Professional tenderness would be acceptable to the surgeon who was now her patient, and he need never suspect that she was in love with him.

She wondered if Trudie l'Estrade had gone home, and hoped, selfishly, that she had gone away for ever. The music started again and she had time to think sadly during the evocative Nocturne that followed. Trudie was a very determined woman and once she thought that any other woman, even a mother, stood between her and the man she had noted down as her own property, that woman would do well to be careful. If she suspected that anyone but her would be there to serve him and gain a fragment of his attention and affection, she would cancel all appointments and fly to his side. Maggie was asking about the beautiful woman she had seen briefly.

'Yes, she dresses expensively and well,' said Nuala. 'Yes, I expect they are all couturier-made,' she said, rapidly becoming tired of the way the conversation was going.

'She'll run to fat,' said Maggie, with malicious satisfaction. 'They do, you know. Have you noted her waist? If she gives up vigorous exercise like ski-ing, she'll be plump in no time.'

Nuala pictured the lovely firm legs and the superb bosom and wondered if that was true. She smiled, hating herself for welcoming the possibility that there might be a fat Trudie lurking in the fine proportions of her figure.

'She looks lovely, now,' said Nuala. And that's what matters. If he sees, no, *when* he sees, he will see her as she is now, in all her beauty, she thought.

'When are you going to be married?' said Maggie, who worried a subject as a dog worries a bone. 'One of the nurses said she saw you with your fiancé. Did he come all this way just to see you?'

'On business,' said Nuala, but Maggie took it that she was being coy.

'Some business,' she said.

'He brought me some things from home and had business in London. I'm not in any hurry to get married yet and he had to go back to Ireland.' She smiled. 'I like it here and I shall stay for a while if Sister French still wants me on her wing.'

The concert ended and they all went back to the hostel. Odinga stayed for only a few minutes to collect more borrowed books and Nuala sighed inwardly as Maggie insisted on making more coffee and talking until late. 'What are you doing tomorrow morning. You do have a long morning off, don't you?'

'I have shopping to do,' said Nuala, firmly. If Maggie talked any more and then wanted to spend the following morning with her, it would be too much. In small slices, she was a good companion, but Nuala wanted to have time to herself. The first cheque had arrived and she wondered what to do with it beyond paying it in to the bank. 'I have to go to the bank and I'm going to buy some shoes,' she said. The sudden awareness that in future she would have money to spend on such things without worrying about the amount left in her account, was just dawning on her, and it helped to take her mind from the cubicle upstairs in the main block.

After a hurried breakfast, taken early to escape Maggie, Nuala caught the bus into the town and found herself window gazing with more enthusiasm than she remembered having for years. The girl in the boutique saw her and smiled, beckoning her in and holding up an armful of summer clothes. 'I didn't come to buy anything, today,' began Nuala, then put out a hand to touch a soft woollen coat of pale green. It was loose fitting and would go happily over both spring and summer clothes, mixing with most colours, and Nuala thought of the soft violet dress hanging in her wardrobe.

As if reading her thoughts, the girl said, 'It would look good with the dress you bought here. With grey high heeled shoes and those nice misty-coloured tights it would be super.'

Nuala left the shop in a daze. She had bought the coat, a light fluffy top and skirt in pale yellow and a sleek cotton suit of coffee linen. On the bus, clutching the many parcels, she smiled. Dear Gran. If I can't have the man I love, you have helped me to know that there are other things in life that I can enjoy.

Once more back in a fresh cool cotton uniform, she felt trim in new sheer black tights and soft black shoes with moderate heels tipped with rubber to make them soundless on tiled floors. The private wing was quiet and the foyer polished brightly. Masses more flowers were on the main table and the newly-delivered ones sat in a double row with cards attached. Instinctively, Nuala bent over to read the cards and to select the blooms intended for Mr Wendover. She picked up an armful, intending to take them with her to arrange as soon as her patient was settled and needed a rest. A message for her asked her to ring a number and as she was assured that it was on official hospital business and not, as she suspected, a call from Dermot, she left the flowers in the sluice room of the wing and went down again to the main foyer as the telephone for Mr Wendover's room was not on the shelf outside.

The telephone rang and rang and then she heard a voice she remembered. 'I'm so glad you rang, Nurse. They told me you were off duty but would be back at two. You're early,' Mrs Wendover said, with evident approval.

'Yes, I'm not due back for ten minutes, but I wanted to be organised before Mr Wendover came back to the room.'

'Oh, he's back. Didn't you know?'

'I've been off duty, specially, so that Sister could have me back here when he was transferred from recovery.' Nuala bit her lip in annoyance. She had wasted a morning on her own frivolous needs when the man she loved and wanted to serve more than any creature on earth, had to put up with anyone who happened to have the time to spare.

'I rang this morning and they told me that he was being taken downstairs again as he wanted to get back to his routine.' She paused. 'This sounds silly, but would you go in to him and tell him that I rang this morning to enquire and to wish him well. I'm at home now and I would like him to ring me here.'

'You could ring now. The telephone is in the room and if he is back you can speak to him directly.' She heard no response. 'I'll go up and if he isn't in any mood or a fit state to take calls, then at least I can give you messages from him.' She thought for a moment. 'You could try now. If there is someone in the room before I get there, they can answer for him.'

'Exactly!'

'Oh, you think he might have a visitor?'

'Almost certainly. I have no intention of telephoning my son and having Trudie l'Estrade telling me what she thinks is best for him. Oh, dear, I sound an absolute Gorgon, don't I?'

'Not a bit. I'd feel the same about anyone I loved. If he's fit to ring you, I'll dial the number and make sure that the call is direct from him to you, but if she's there, I may have to play it by ear and wait a little.'

'I shall wait. I don't mind how long I wait, but if the call is impossible to make, could you ring me from the office?' Her voice was wistful and Nuala felt a surge of anger that the lovely Trudie should try to shut out anyone but her, in the life of the surgeon who was as yet not in full control of his affairs.

'If you haven't heard during the next half an hour, I'll slip down to reception as soon as I can to give you an up-to-date bulletin about his condition.'

'Bless you. What a dear person you are. I wondered . . .'

'Yes?' Nuala made her voice encouraging.

'Tomorrow, if you are off duty, could you see

me? There might be matters concerning my son that we need to talk about and it would be so much easier over a cup of coffee.'

'If you want that, I could meet you during the afternoon for tea in that nice new tea shop. Would that do?'

'I shall look forward to that more than you can know. It's nearly two. I mustn't make trouble for you with your seniors, dear. Goodbye.'

The rest of the flowers joined those on the table in the sluice room and Nuala straightened her skirt and hair as she tapped on the closed door.

The room was empty. Her heart lurched at the thought that he might have been taken back to the operating theatre for more emergency treatment and she hurried along to Sister French in her office. It was stupid to panic. There must be many simple explanations for his absence from his room even after she was convinced that he had been transferred there.

'Reporting back, Sister,' she said. 'I heard that my patient was back, but the room is empty.'

'And you thought the worst? Did you think he'd been abducted or discharged himself?'

'I did expect to find him, Sister.' Her beating heart regained its normal rhythm. Sister French was smiling, slightly, but trying to sound official.

'Mr Micheljon wanted to put in more drops, so we took him back upstairs for a while.'

'But why? We have all the equipment here and the wing is quieter than the six-bedded room.'

'Not this morning, it wasn't!'

'I don't understand.'

'Miss l'Estrade came almost as soon as he was

back in his room. She talked far too much for a first visit after a traumatic experience and Mr Micheljon popped in to see if he was settling and decided, tactfully, to take him away again for a while.'

'Did Mr Wendover object?'

'He was the perfect patient,' she said dryly. 'Told her to go and have lunch and went like a lamb, murmuring apologies about trying to get back here too soon.'

'And now?'

'You can hear the lift? He's coming back. I told him that you would be here to welcome him at two.'

'And Miss l'Estrade?'

'She'll be back,' she said, and Nuala thought that there was a hint of disapproval in Sister's voice. 'She was very cross because he wasn't ready to give her his full attention. She was almost rude to Mr Micheljon, saying that she had cancelled one flight in order to see him and now had to waste time away from him. She wanted to know when he would be fit to fly out to Geneva with her.'

'She can't expect him to travel yet?'

'That's what Mr Micheljon said.' The lift gates opened and closed at the end of the corridor. 'You're right, Nurse. He can't fly off across Europe with a woman who has no experience of nursing or surgical care, but that young woman is very domineering and I had to hold my peace or I would have said more than was good for the hospital.' She glanced at Nuala, as if to make sure that she had received the message that reticence must be observed in all her dealings with patients and visitors. Geneva? Of course he would go away to Geneva as soon as he could travel, but Nuala was certain as a nurse that he was not ready to go away, to a sighted world, when his own eyes were covered and he had no education in the ways of the poorly sighted, or the blind. The woman in her who loved him wanted to cry that he must stay, for a while longer, so that she could care for him in the only way he would ever need her, as a devoted and efficient nurse.

'I'll be very careful what I say,' she promised, and saw the wheelchair coming round the bend of the corridor, with a man sitting in it. At the doorway to the room, Sister French put a hand on the man's arm. He looked magnificent in a dressing gown of dark blue silk, with most impressive dragons decorating the sleeves and back of the garment. Nuala couldn't help smiling. He looked like a pet dragon, as yet he wasn't breathing fire, but he sat straight with his hands on the chair, gripping it tightly.

'Just because I'm a bit unsteady at present, is it necessary to put me in this thing, Sister?'

'I'm sure they did what they considered right, Mr Wendover,' Sister said, mildly.

'I can walk from here,' he said, curtly. 'I'm not a cripple, and now they've done their worst, I'm allowed to move a few inches on my own.'

Suddenly, he's embarrassed, thought Nuala. Although he knows that both Sister and I have seen him in many more upsetting situations when he was ill, he's self-conscious about being in a wheelchair. The thought was a shock. He would want to be free of all help, now. He would say that he had no further use for a special nurse. 'Thank you for all you've done for me, Nurse', with perhaps a small gift in recognition of her efforts. Her mouth was dry. He would reduce her to just another member of staff who did her work adequately and made everything easy for her patient.

'We can help you to walk,' she said.

'Ah, Nurse Kavanagh. Do you really feel strong enough?' The mockery tore at her heart, dismissing her again as the small nurse who had been concerned for him but who had been unable to prevent his injury. Would he ever recall the full record of events that night?

'But you did say you came from a wiry family. I can manage.' He stood up, sending the wheelchair backwards towards the bend in the corridor where the stairs appeared. It ran full-tilt into the person who had been forced to climb the stairs as the lift doors were open.

'Oh, No! Miss l'Estrade,' said Nuala, unsure if she should run to her or to attend the man with his hand firmly on her shoulder. His grip tightened and she had to stay. She glanced up at his face and had a sneaking suspicion that he was smiling.

Sister French rushed to help the woman who was struggling to her feet, but she was pushed aside, furiously. Sister retrieved the chair and locked it by the stairs while Trudie l'Estrade brushed down her skirt.

'I am not hurt, I hurried back from lunch and the lift is not working. It is very bad,' she said, then her voice took on a warm and loving note. 'My darling Blake,' she said, coming towards him, her high heels tap-tapping on the tiled floor. 'It is wonderful to see you walking again.' She pushed Nuala rudely away and took his hand. 'I will help you, Blake. I came just in time, *n'est ce pas*? We will walk together, you and I, for we have much to discuss.'

'I will open the door. I think you should sit down in your room quietly for a while,' said Sister French. Trudie looked sulky, but Blake Wendover turned to the door and Trudie went with him, clutching the green dragon on his right arm. Nuala followed, feeling useless, and Trudie tried to shut the door before either of the nursing staff could follow, but Sister French took the door firmly and held it until the patient was in his big chair. She told Nuala to go in and read out the new messages that had arrived with the flowers and even Trudie couldn't send her away.

Nuala was acutely aware of the resentful glance that followed her. She knew that her improved appearance would find no favour with the beautiful Swiss girl, and wondered if that made her sound spiteful. 'There is a card from Mrs Wendover and she asked if you would telephone her. The telephone is there at your elbow and I have the number here ready for you, if you can't remember it.' Trudie made a movement from her chair by the window, but Nuala continued, 'She said that she is rather tired of speaking through a third person and would like to hear your voice as soon as you are fit to talk to her.'

'He is tired. You heard the sister say that he must rest. I will make the call,' said Trudie. 'There is no need for you to do anything to tire you, my darling,' she said.

'You heard what Nurse Kavanagh said. I must ring her. I promised to do so as soon as I was certain of my fate.'

'Your fate?' Trudie sounded less confident. 'Blake, my darling, do not use such words, it sounds bad.'

'And if it is bad, Trudie?' His face was suddenly tense and hard. 'What if I say to you that now they have done everything possible for me, I shall make no further progress? What if I say that I have no further treatment and am to be discharged?'

Nuala held on to the bed table and hardly dared to breathe in case she sobbed aloud. His face was set and his mouth gave a hint of great tension. A third person had no right to witness this scene.

'It is not true. Tell me it is not bad.' She laughed, with a brittle sound. 'It cannot be true. If you could not see, you would have to have a guide all the time, a nurse to be with you or an assistant to help you.'

The dark glasses turned away and, if he had been able to see, his gaze would have rested on the girl who stood so silently and frozen-faced with agony. 'I am very glad about one thing, Trudie,' he said. 'I have never actually asked you to marry me.' She looked annoyed. 'I have not asked you, and, of course, I could not ask you now. The burden of a bad-tempered husband would never come up to your expectations of what a marriage should be.'

'But we understand one another, Blake. My family think you are suitable for me and I love you.'

'And yet, we have never become engaged to be married,' he said, firmly.

'We must talk more,' she said. 'I have to speak to my brother.'

'I could never trap any woman into a marriage that would not fulfil her dearest hopes,' he said, quietly. 'Life with me would not be to your liking, my dear. I think you should go down to reception and book the next flight out to Geneva and see your family. They will be glad to have your company and I hear the ski runs are good.'

'And you cannot *ski*?' The full force of the situation struck her for the first time. Trudie gave him a look that was almost tinged with dislike. 'I must think. What you say is right. We are not bound by vows and you need time to get used to being as you are. I will go back and think of you. I will pray for a miracle for you and we must make sure that you have every attention, always.'

She was gathering up her mink jacket and the Gucci handbag. The thick blonde hair was thrust into a soft wool and mink hat. If he could see her now, he would break his heart to know that he is losing her, thought Nuala, forgetting her own pain in his terrible self-control.

'You will have a nurse to look after you until I see you again?' Trudie looked at Nuala and smiled. 'This little one might do well. She is quiet and useful and you have no need to look on anyone pretty now, until the miracle happens and I come back for you.'

Nuala blushed. How dared she speak like that, as if the nurse had no feelings? How could the woman go away when he needed her. If I loved and was loved, I would give everything in love and service for a lifetime. I could never walk out on someone who needed me, she thought furiously.

Trudie went over and kissed Blake Wendover on the cheek. 'I must go. I have missed a plane to stay with you, but it is not important.' It sounded as if she had made a great sacrifice. She went to the door. 'I will write to you, often.' She frowned. 'That might be bad. I do not want my letters read by another person. I will be in touch, because I do not believe that you can never see. I shall talk to my brothers and they will see you and bring you to Switzerland for treatment.' She seemed to gain confidence again. 'It will all be well, but we have to be patient, my darling.'

The heavy perfume left a trail of musk as she went into the corridor and the tap of her heels receded to the lift. Blake Wendover seemed to relax. He smiled. 'I'd like to speak to my mother alone, if you don't mind, Nurse Kavanagh,' he said. 'Then, I'd like a quiet cup of tea.'

'Of course,' was all she could find to say. The poor brave man had the awful task of breaking the news to his mother that the woman he loved had gone away and it might be for ever unless he recovered his full sight. He needed company and must be made to forget the heartless woman who had left him. 'I'll dial the number for you,' she said, and waited to make sure it was ringing.

'Has she really gone?' Sister French looked slightly ruffled.' I don't know when I've been more irritated by a woman. A couple of days' rest and he'll be confident enough to go to his mother. We want him to do as much as possible for himself now to get him used to being in the outside world again.'

Nuala knew that this was the only sane approach. It would be harmful if everyone wept over him. There had been no firm statement about his condition, but she knew that patients on the private wing often made it clear that they wished their state of health to be treated as confidential and only the nurses involved in their individual care, or the sister in charge, knew the details. Nuala had the feeling that Mr Wendover wanted to tell his friends about himself in his own words and in his own time. Even I know nothing of what was said when the last examination was made, she thought. I heard only his rather cryptic comment that there would be no further treatment and he could expect no real change in his condition. His dark glasses might be the precursor to gradual use of pin holes of light and one eye might have recovered in time, but that was in the future.

What matters now, she decided, was to make sure that he didn't feel that everyone pitied him. She wondered what he was saying to his mother on the telephone. It was bad enough to have to tell her that his eyes would not improve further than they had done with treatment, but to have to admit that the woman he loved and needed had taken him at his word when he made the sacrifice of saying that he could never marry her and bring this burden on a bright and active life, was shattering to a man of his pride.

Sister French was called away before Nuala could ask any questions about him, so the flowers were her only task and she went to arrange them until the bell rang and she went to see her patient. The tea tray was lying on the table by the window and Nuala knew that he must have walked there to put it there, unless the junior who was taking teas round, had put it there by mistake while he was using the telephone.

'I've finished my chat,' he said. 'Mattie said thank you for organising the call.'

'I did nothing,' she said. 'You would have called her without any prompting from me.'

'You made it easier,' he said, and smiled. 'It didn't please Trudie, I'm afraid, but she has always been a bossy little thing.'

Nuala couldn't help smiling. Imagine anyone calling the poised and beautiful girl a bossy little thing as if she was all pig-tails and hockey sticks. She heard him sigh and ached for his sorrow. 'Are you tired?' she said. 'Why not have a nap before supper?'

'Determined to tuck me up nice and warm, even if it might be for the last time?'

'I have to look after you while you are in my care,' she said.

'And you would never leave anyone before the need for your tender loving care had gone, would you, Nurse Nuala?'

She picked up the huge bouquet that had come from Trudie that day and hid her face in it, although she knew he couldn't see her through the staring black lenses.

'I would not,' she said, with more vehemence than she intended.

'No, you wouldn't,' he said, in a curiously flat voice. 'What are you going to do now while I rest?'

'I still have masses of flowers out there as well as this lovely bouquet from Miss l'Estrade.'

'Take them all down to the geriatric ward.'

'All of them?'

'All of them and any that come while I'm here.

I'm not going to die, you know, and I feel as if I'm surrounded by wreaths.'

'I'll take them now unless you need any help?'

'None, thank you. Just take the flowers and then come and read to me, for the last time. I'm going out soon, you know.'

'Yes, I did hear that much,' she said, hoping that he would confide in her about his condition.

He ignored the implied question. 'I may not see you again if they send you to another department.'

'Have you made arrangements for when you leave?'

'All settled. Mattie doesn't approve of all of them, but I have to make my own decisions. I hope to travel again soon.'

'You do?'

'I thought that Switzerland might be good for a brief holiday this summer. It's beautiful in summer.'

'I can guess,' she said, in little more than a whisper. How could he talk of travelling when he might see nothing, or see everything through a mist? It was slightly unnerving to be stared at by dark glasses, as if the eyes behind them could see. Nuala felt exposed and edged towards the door. Switzerland would mean Trudie. Was he so in love that he would follow her even if he couldn't marry her?

She took away the flowers and the tea-tray and went down to the ward with the lovely blooms, to the delight of the old ladies there. It took longer than she had intended and when she went back and tapped gently on the door there was no reply. She tip-toed in and saw that Blake Wendover was lying on the top of the bed, still in his dragon gown, and he was fast asleep.

She touched his cheek, softly, and he stirred but didn't wake. 'Goodbye, Blake,' she murmured, and went out softly to Sister French and her future instructions.

CHAPTER EIGHT

THE draught from the swing doors was as Nuala recalled from her first period of work in Out-patients, but that seemed light years away and she was miserable. She shivered slightly and decided to go over to her room at the first opportunity to put a warm thin woolly under her cotton dress, but as she saw the steady stream of patients walking into the gastro-intestinal clinic at St Jude's hospital, she knew that there would be little time to spare.

'Nurse Kavanagh?' That voice hadn't changed, either. Sister Frazer was carrying a pile of X-rays and notes and Nuala cleared a space for them quickly as she saw her approach. 'Thank you, Nurse,' she said, grudgingly, and let them flop on to the desk in an untidy pile. 'Get that lot sorted, Nurse, and make sure everyone has his or her notes ready for the surgeon when their name is called.'

'Yes, Sister.' That reply was the same, too, and it was the one that echoed round the department all day. Yes, Sister, no, Sister—it was hopeless to argue and quicker to agree with everything she said. Sister Frazer looked at the notes as if she had never seen them but wondered who could have made them so untidy. Any minute now she'll hint that I left them like that, thought Nuala, and began to sort them out, putting X-rays with the relevant notes and having a notepad handy to jot down any that seemed to be missing. This clinic was for people already examined by the consultant in diseases of the stomach and intestines. They had been X-rayed and tested in various ways and now reported back to be assessed for bed care, operation or discharge from the clinic as cured or at least with their condition controlled.

'There are three X-rays missing, Sister. It seems likely that these three patients have had them done as they were due for barium meal.'

Sister Frazer clucked with annoyance. 'Well, you'd better do something about it, Nurse.'

What does she expect, thought Nuala resentfully as she hurried up to X-ray to fetch the plates. Anyone would think I had given the barium meals and forgotten to take the pictures. In one way, this tension was good. There was no time to stand about and dream, and certainly no time for tears. It had been a shock to be told to report back to the Outpatients as soon as she appeared in the dining room for breakfast the day after she learned that Blake Wendover was leaving the private wing. All that night, she had consoled herself with the thought that she would be able to say goodbye to him, but she had not gone back to the wing. Fortunately, there was no clinic during the afternoon and Sister wanted her back for the evening in Casualty, so her tea-date with his mother was safe.

After a gruelling morning when nothing seemed to go right, Nuala went to lunch and off duty for the afternoon. Sister French caught up with her as she reached the cafeteria. 'I'm sorry to lose you, Nurse,' she said. 'I did make quite a fuss, but as Mr Wendover no longer needs a special, I had to let you go, at least for a time.' She smiled, apologetically. 'I did insist that you kept your day off in two days' time, and I hope that your other arrangements are safe?'

'Yes, thank you, Sister. I can't say I was overjoyed to go back, but they are short of staff.' She tried to sound casual. 'What of Mr Wendover, Sister?'

'Oh, he'll be fine. He is going home in those rather sexy dark glasses. I told him he looks like an important member of the Mafia. He's done a lot of telephoning as he insisted on telling everyone about himself rather than letting them learn indirectly. What did he say to you last night?' Sister asked.

'Not a lot,' said Nuala. 'He was asleep when I got back to make sure he was comfortable, and I didn't see him again.'

'No, I suppose there wasn't much to say. It could all be said in a few words and we're glad it's over and he's been so patient. I'm not sure where Miss l'Estrade fits in, now. Are they engaged? He spoke of going to Switzerland, so that must mean he'll be with her. She kept on about it enough. She seemed to need to convince herself that she really was engaged to him,' added Sister, with a frown. 'Strange, really. All that heel-tapping when the rugs were being cleaned would have driven most men mad. I was a little worried in case she made his condition worse. Stress can do nasty things and the optic nerve could become more sensitive again. It's amazing how an injured eye can make the other one behave in the same manner out of sympathy. I know that I cry in smypathy if I see someone with watering eyes. I'd be hopeless in an eye theatre.'

Nuala wanted to scream, I know about that, but

it doesn't help Blake, does it? How can you be so
calm about a man who has to make a new life
without the love of the woman he wants? But she
managed to smile, weakly, and go in to lunch. All
she wanted to do was to eat her food and then sink
down on her bed for the afternoon, but she had
promised to meet Mrs Wendover. Nuala wondered
if she should telephone in case it was now inconve-
nient to meet her if Blake Wendover insisted on
being discharged today. But no call came for her
and she found herself dressing with care in the new
violet-coloured dress and the warm coat she had
bought in the boutique. Although the wind was
gusty, there was no sign of rain, so she set out for
the tea shop with confidence, under the pale blue
skies and clouds scudding in wisps above the trees.

The small tea room had been open for only a few
weeks and was deliberately old-fashioned, from the
dark oak furniture to the pretty embroidered nap-
kins and table clothes and silver butter dishes.
There were a few people eating scones and jam and
pastries, but no woman sitting alone. Nuala sat by
the window and waited, saying that she would
order later, but half expecting that Mrs Wendover
would have forgotten her in the excitement of her
son's homecoming.

She had almost decided to order a pot of tea and
a toasted tea cake when the door opened and a very
elegant woman with curly grey hair and wide grey
eyes came into the room. She looked round at the
customers and came towards Nuala. 'You must be
Nuala,' she said.

'Yes, I'm Nuala Kavanagh,' said the girl, shyly.
'How did you know?'

Mrs Wendover smiled. 'I always did like violet,' she said, which was no reason at all, thought Nuala.

They ordered tea, and made conversation about the weather, the tea shop and the colour of Nuala's dress, in fact they talked about everything but the subject on their minds, Blake Wendover. 'You look just as you sound on the telephone,' said Nuala, finding it easy to talk to the woman who knew Blake more than any person alive.

'And you are just as I was given to expect,' said Mattie.

'Mrs Wendover,' began Nuala.

'Call me Mattie. I have so little time to get to know you and we must make the most of it. Blake told me of your care and devotion and I am very glad to meet you.

Nuala sipped her tea and hid her eyes from the kind but penetrating gaze. 'I *am* a nurse,' she said.

'That comes second to being a very sweet human being.' Nuala couldn't think that Blake Wendover had said that and smiled. Mattie had her own very definite ideas about people. 'Not like one lady I know,' said Mattie, with a glint in her eyes. 'I shall be glad when that young woman has gone back to Switzerland.'

'But she left yesterday.' Nuala sat up straight, her cheeks flaming. 'She was on her way to the airport.'

'No, she couldn't get a flight at once, so she rang her brother in Geneva.'

'You've seen her?'

'She is listening to the foreign news in my flat at this moment,' she said, with an audible sigh. 'Unfortunately, my dear son telephoned once too often. He rang Marc, Trudie's brother, who is a good friend, and he told him that he hoped to be in Switzerland soon.'

'He rang before Miss l'Estrade telephoned Geneva?' said Nuala. 'So she knows that he means to go there after her?' She couldn't hide the pain in her voice.

'That's what she thinks,' said Mattie. She regarded Nuala with a long cool appraisal, as if her reaction to the news was important. 'Do you think she is in love with my son?'

'I think she was in love with the man who . . . before the accident. I don't think she could cope with a man who didn't follow the same pursuits as she does,' said Nuala, trying not to sound too unfair. 'Some people really find it impossible to be concerned about illness. I think she must be like that.'

'How tactful,' said Mattie. 'I'm afraid I'd be far less charitable. I told her just before I left that I didn't want her as a daughter-in-law at any price and that the sooner she went home, the better I would be pleased.' Mattie looked serious.

'You didn't!' said Nuala, aghast at the courage of a woman who could confront Trudie l'Estrade.

'I also think I might have told her a lie. I said that Blake was in love with another woman and that he would marry nobody until he was sure of his sight.'

'His sight? The other eye might be saved?'

'Blake made me promise to discuss that with no one.'

'But he didn't say anything and Sister French thought he had told me all there was to know.'

'He has one more check before we know everything.' She shrugged. 'The line was bad to Geneva and Marc had the impression that Blake could see. That's what made Trudie come hot-foot to me, in a terrible rage, complaining that she should have been told the news first.'

'And is she going away?'

'Her flight leaves tonight. She wanted to see Blake, but I'm afraid I refused to tell her where he is staying. He left the wing this morning and he wants to be alone for a while.'

'But who will look after him? He shouldn't be alone. What if he hurts himself?'

'I agree. He shouldn't be alone, ever. He has gone to his own home. Don't look surprised. You didn't think we lived together, did you? That would be stupid. We are very good friends, but we need our own spaces. In my business, I have to be mobile and everyone comes to see me. Blake has a similar set-up, but they don't coincide very well. I adore him, but I don't want to live with him. He will be fine. I believe he has a sort of housekeeper who lives out. She will look after him. He looked well, this morning, didn't you think?'

'I didn't see him. He was asleep last night and I was sent to another department this morning.'

'But he sent you a message to go to see him before he left.' She looked concerned. 'You didn't get the message?' Nuala shook her head. 'Oh, dear, I know he wanted to see you.'

Nuala fought to control her anger. It must have been Sister Frazer who took the message and didn't pass it on. Seldom had Nuala hated anyone as she hated Sister Frazer at that moment. 'We were very busy, and Sister is a little vague at times,' she said.

'Will you explain to Mr Wendover when you see him?'

'I'll speak to him,' she said. They left the tea shop and parted by the car park where Mattie had left her car. Nuala refused the offer of a lift, saying that it wasn't far to walk and that she wanted some fresh air before she went back on duty for the evening.

'Don't let them work you too hard, dear. I hope we meet again, soon,' said Mattie.

Nuala smiled and there were tears in her eyes as she turned away. I shall be unlikely to meet her again, she thought, with regret. If Blake Wendover is in love with another woman, she must be wonderful if he prefers her to Trudie. She wondered where the other girl lived and if he had been so in love that he had said nothing to her about his operation and so she had no chance to visit him. It would account for the fact that he was so firm in his manner when he said that Trudie and he had never been engaged. How awkward it must have been for him to know that he was in love with someone and that Trudie looked on him as her property.

This other love must be worthy of him. Nuala couldn't decide if she was glad or sorry. If she loved him and cared for him, there could never be any need of a little Irish nurse in his life. If she was like Trudie, he would suffer. Neither answer was good and she walked slowly back to the hospital, wondering what would become of the man she loved.

'Did you get your package?' said Sister Odinga as they met at supper?

'Package? No, I haven't been to collect my letters today.'

'Feeling worn out after another day in Out-patients?'

'Something like that,' said Nuala.

'Cheer up, we'll make coffee as soon as we come off duty. I seem to be in your place more than my own at the moment. Most of my friends live there and it's so convenient.' She laughed. 'I've been shopping. Every time I buy something pretty, I convince myself that it's for my trousseau and then I find that I just have to wear it.'

The fact that she had finished a very busy day was useful in hiding the weariness of her soul. If she looked drained, everyone would think that it was Sister Frazer and her bullying and have no suspicion that there could be another cause. 'One more day before my day off,' Nuala said. 'I must have gone soft working in PP wing with all that warmth and carpeting. The wind whistles round the old block like a demon with knives.'

'I must be mad to stay in this country,' said Odinga. 'I say that when it rains, as it did just now, but when it's sunny and the leaves are green, I love it. Have you seen the pink blossom and the yellow forsythia? It seems to flourish in every back garden I see.'

'Nice,' said Nuala, without enthusiasm. They walked across to the lodge by the doctors' car park to collect mail and the parcel that Odinga had left there on her way back on duty. From habit, Nuala glanced towards the corner where Blake Wendover had left his big black car on the day when he was admitted to hospital for treatment to his eyes. He had driven the car early in the day, but as his sight deteriorated and he was admitted to the private patient wing, it had remained there awaiting collection. Dust and small green leaves from the overhanging trees had covered the shining top and it had begun to look forlorn. Today, as Nuala looked across the car park, there was an empty space. She stared. A cold splash of water went into her shoe from one of the puddles on the drive. A neat rectangle of dry gravel showed where the car had been, and as the rest of the car park was soaking from the one severe wetting it had received that day, late in the afternoon, the car must have been there until quite recently.

'I saw the car go when I was in Ward Four, but I couldn't see who drove it away. I heard that his mother was in the building earlier, so she might have taken it. Did you see him to say goodbye?'

'No,' said Nuala. 'He sent a message, but Sister forgot to give it to me.'

'I didn't see him either. I had the feeling that he wanted to go without fuss.' Sister Odinga frowned. 'Not like him, really, all this hush-hush about his condition. I know that the wing is very cagey about telling any details to outsiders, but he is worse than any film star having a face lift!'

'I think he needs time to sort out who are his real friends,' said Nuala. 'Trudje has almost said that she doesn't want him if he can't see enough to ski, but she hung on until the last minute in case she could find out more.'

'Well, she'd be a fool to let him go,' said Odinga. 'As well as being a very attractive man, he is very prosperous and a good catch for anyone.'

Nuala picked up her letters and a small package,

then changed into a housecoat and slippers and went down to the sitting-room to make coffee. The first letter, which she read as they waited for the coffee to filter, was from her mother. There was guarded pleasure about the legacy that her daughter had been left, but underlying it all was disapproval stemming from Nuala's rejection of Dermot. 'Of course, now that you are determined to be an old maid, you'll sell the house. It would be much too big for you unless you settle there and take in patients for a living.'

It seemed sad to think that the dear old house couldn't be used again for a family, or for lots of families as a holiday home, and her mother's dictatorial tone made Nuala resolve to keep the decision until later and to hang on to her property until she knew that her final choice was the right one. It was an extravagance to keep it, but she couldn't bear the thought of anyone who didn't care about the house ruining it. The old lady had much loved old furniture which would suffer under the heedlessness of sticky-fingered children, people bringing in sea shells and sand and leaving them in the hall to be trampled into the carpets and casual tenants who would let the old-world garden run to seed.

She put the letter aside and saw the package lying unopened by the coffee pot. It might be a gift from Dermot, hoping to smooth over their parting, making overtures that might re-admit him to the good graces of the girl who was now worth his notice. A catalogue from a dress firm found a ready home with a girl who liked to buy her clothes by mail order, but spent a fortune on sending back those that didn't fit, much to the amusement of her friends who couldn't convince her that she was not buying a bargain.

Odinga showed off her buys and the ring given to her by her fiancé. 'We've decided to marry before he finishes his course,' she said. 'We can live together at weekends or when I have time off. It will be a series of honeymoons.'

Nuala smiled, trying to feel joy for her friend. 'I ought to go to bed,' she said. 'Sister Frazer will be breathing down my neck tomorrow and I shall need all my strength.'

'Which clinic?'

'Fractures in the morning and Skins in the afternoon,' said Nuala with a groan. 'I hate all that plaster of Paris slopping about the place. One of the men still uses old Cellona bandages and he doesn't care where he splashes it. It never comes off if it isn't wiped up at once, and if the nurse is away when the plaster is applied, the wretched stuff is hard before she comes back.'

'You'll be busy. It's always bad after a cold spell. They'll all be there ready to have a change of plaster if they fell during that last icy week.'

'Thanks a lot! That's all I need.' She said goodnight and went to her room. The package sat on the table, with no address on it, and no post mark. Her name was neatly written in capitals and it was featureless. It couldn't have come from Dermot, but she had no energy left to think about it and less still to open it. She went to sleep with the thought that Mrs Wendover had promised to ring her and they might possibly meet again. It doesn't help, seeing the same level gaze from the eyes of his mother, she thought, but at least I shall feel slightly less cut off from him until I get used to this perpetual ache when I think of him. Had she ever read poetry to him without weeping? The memory of those precious sessions would stay with her for ever and as she slept she found her eyes wet with memory. The package stayed forgotten on the table as she went to bed, exhausted.

CHAPTER NINE

Nuala stood in a huge rubber apron that sounded like a boat under sail as she walked about the department. House surgeons and registrars were busy removing old plasters, sending patients for X-rays and re-applying casts when necessary. By noon, the line of new plasters by the radiators had grown, as the injured sat waiting to dry off enough to go home or to have rocker bars or rubber heels fitted to the hard plasters, and the chairs of people waiting were nearly empty.

It hadn't been as bad as Nuala had expected. Sister Frazer had been busy with one of the consultants and the registrar was in a good mood. Nothing calamitous had happened and Nuala felt better. As lunch time approached, aprons were peeled off, floors swabbed and the cubicles made ready for the afternoon clinic. Sister sent Nuala to lunch, after telling her to go and change her tights which had traces of fast-hardening plaster on them, even though she had worn theatre boots for the worst of the plastering.

Sister seemed uneasy. 'I'm sorry, Nurse, but I believe I forgot to give you a message,' she said.

'If it was to say goodbye to Mr Wendover, it isn't important, Sister. He left before I could see him, yesterday.' She was determined to show no reaction.

'Oh!' said Sister Frazer. 'I forgot that, too, but,

as you know, we were much too busy for you to leave the department on such a frivolous errand. It doesn't do for nurses to become sentimental over staff,' she said, with a sniff.

'The other message, Sister?' Nuala looked at her with cool hazel eyes. 'If I could know what that one was, I will at least be in the position to apologise if I can't keep that appointment, either.'

Sister looked at her sharply, wondering at the cold note in the normally soft voice. 'I have a telephone number for you to ring. I suppose you can ring now in the annexe, although, as you insist on taking your day off tomorrow, it could have waited.'

Nuala glanced at the number, and her heart missed a beat. Mattie hadn't forgotten her. It was the telephone number of her flat. Nuala half-smiled, 'Thank you, Sister.'

'A call from your family?'

'No, Sister,' was all she would say.

She took off the soiled tights as soon as she got to her room, then saw the package. Half intrigued, she opened it and the outer brown paper came away to reveal the distinctive wrapping of the store where she had bought the perfume for Blake to give to Trudie. How naive I am, she thought. I really should try to look beyond the obvious. She took out the very same bottle that she had chosen with Sister Odinga such a short time ago. Her lower lip trembled. Perhaps, for once, she had looked beyond the obvious when she had wondered if the parting with Blake would be a cool thank you and a small gift as a sign that, whatever had happened, the period in hospital was over and he was going on to other people, other ties. No note with it, not even a card. He must have wanted no other nurse to know that he gave presents to staff, or he would have asked a nurse to write on a card for her.

It was a strange feeling to know that, even after being with him so closely, he didn't know her. He had only seen her face in a situation not likely to imprint her on his memory, and again when he was suffering from slight amnesia and profound shock. He knew that she was Irish, had a soft voice and manner, walked quietly and fed him with care, respecting his wishes when he wanted to be alone or quiet, when he wanted her to talk or read to him and when he needed her physical help. She tried to imagine him with sight, walking by in the corridor and not knowing that the nurse with the hazel eyes and powdering of freckles was the nurse who read poetry. He might come back for check-ups and not spare a glance for her. If she kept silent, he would not know the girl who had rested his head on her shoulder when she arranged his pillows.

The bottle was on the dressing table unopened. There would be time enough for that when the raw edges of her spirit were healed or at least safe in deep scars. She dialled the number of Mattie's flat and wondered what was left to say to the mother of the man she loved but could never marry.

The pleasant voice seemed glad to hear from her. 'I was hoping you'd ring now. I have several business meetings during the next few days and I wanted to get my diary straight. I want to see you again, soon, Nuala. Could you manage tomorrow evening? We could have dinner together and I can tell you all the news.'

'What news?' Nuala couldn't keep the eagerness from her voice.

'I can't stop to tell you now, but I will say that Trudie has gone. She is convinced that Blake is in love with someone and as I wouldn't say who that might be, she went off to Geneva in a fine old temper, but I did give her a name of a very attractive man in my own kind of business in clothes and couture design. More her type and he likes blondes,' she added, airily. 'I think they might be good for each other.'

'Do you always match-make? Let's hope that Trudie agrees with you this time.'

'Whatever makes you think I'm a devious old soul?' said Mattie with a chuckle. 'I like to see people happy. Shall we say seven-thirty at the Dragon and Horse? I'll book a table.'

Nuala walked back from lunch with Sister Odinga. 'I don't really want to go,' she said. 'I've finished nursing her son and she's already thanked me. He sent me that perfume we bought that day, so he's done his part in saying thanks and goodbye.' Her face gave nothing away, but Odinga glanced at her anxiously. 'We shall have no further contact as it is hospital policy to discourage friendships between staff and patients.'

'But you like his mother. Don't you want to have her as a friend?'

'Of course I do,' said Nuala, warmly. 'She's a wonderful person, but it could be embarrassing if Mr Wendover came along when I was with her. It would seem very strange. Do you realise, he doesn't know me? If his sight has improved, enough to let him see me, it would mean nothing. I have been a voice and that's all.'

'I know what the hospital teaching is, but it doesn't apply here. Blake is a member of staff, not just a patient. He isn't an ordinary member of staff, either. He's much more. As a senior member of surgery, it was an honour to nurse him. He's also a very good friend of mine and I'd hate you to hurt his mother by not going to have dinner with her.' Sister Odinga was serious. 'I love that man,' she said.

'I still feel embarrassed. He left me the scent with no note or card, as if he wanted to throw it at me! I think he was very upset because I witnessed the scene between him and Trudie l'Estrade when she walked out on him. He was being so controlled, so wonderful. It must have broken his heart, but he was quite calm. If he sees me . . . I mean if he has any further contact with me, it will open the wounds and give him pain.'

'Anyone would think you were meeting him and not his mother. What are you worrying about? Meet her and enjoy her company. You'll have a very good dinner at the Dragon and Horse.' Odinga laughed. 'I shall come to your room tomorrow at six and make sure you get ready for the evening. It's no use trying to get out of it. I say that you will go!'

And Odinga was as good as her word. Nuala smiled when the determined tapping on her door wouldn't stop until she had an answer. Nuala opened the door, her hair curling in the steam from the shower and her dressing gown belted.

'If I go tonight, he might think we are discussing him behind his back,' said Nuala.

'Stupid! Sometimes, Nuala Kavanagh, I despair of you. If someone offered me dinner at that good restaurant, I would go even if I was bored to death. I'd go if I had to eat with Dracula. I know it's almost on his door step, but you won't see him if he's having a meal there. The medics go to the bar for Inn Food when they meet to talk shop.'

'I don't know what to wear. I can't wear jeans, can I? But it's going to rain.'

'You'll wear that pretty dress again.'

'I can't wear the coat if it rains,' said Nuala, trying to clutch at her independence. Mattie had asked her to wear that dress when they spoke on the telephone and here was Odinga saying the same. 'I'll wear the dress and put my mac over it.' She looked through the window at the scudding clouds. 'Pity about the shoes, but light grey would mark badly in the rain. One puddle in the drive and I'd be soaked.'

'My dear girl, I shall hit you if you don't get moving. I am going to ring for a taxi right now and you just be good and ready when I come back, or I'll spank you.'

Nuala smiled. 'All right, I'll do as I'm told, as usual.' She went to the wardrobe and found the violet dress. The soft material was warm and cling-ing and felt good as she slipped it over her head, pulling it down over her slim hips. Her hair was right with the dress and she wondered why she had resisted for so long the urge to have her hair styled. She applied make-up carefully and lightly, accen-tuating the eyes and softening the freckles. A rosy lipstick picked up the glow of the dress and she clasped a pendant of amethyst and pearls round her neck to fall over the rise of her breast. She hesitated before her usual scent spray, then tore open the new bottle. *I can tell his mother I am wearing it,* making it seem a pleasant thought remembered, and she can say if she likes his choice, and after today, they will both have done their well-bred duty and in months to come they will have forgotten my existence.

The girl who stared at her from the mirror seemed oddly defiant, as if daring anyone to forget her. He might remember that at some time round St Patrick's Day, a nurse had given him a sprig of shamrock for good luck, if he knows the date or sees the shamrock being worn. She checked her bag and money in case she had to have a taxi home after dinner, because the grey shoes must be protected. *What an extravagant girl I'm becoming,* she thought, *wearing delicate shoes in bad weather and taking taxis.*

'You look very good. Turn around.' Odinga smoothed the back of the pale green coat and untwisted the belt. 'You'll have to watch that. I have one that does the same, or did you get it in a twist because you are scared?'

'Why should I be scared? As you say, she's doing the civilised thing in inviting me and I expect that Sister French will have a similar invitation soon.'

'Wait downstairs until the cab comes.'

'Yes, ma'am,' said Nuala, meekly. She picked her way over the uneven doorstep and climbed into the cab, giving the name of the hotel as she sat down.

They passed along by the river and the pub where she went sometimes with some of the nurses and students. The bridge led to the older part of the town that had sprung up round a few houses of dignity and beauty, not quite submerging the elegance of a time when each of the houses was surrounded by its own spacious grounds, in proud isolation. In one of these houses, now made into luxury flats, Blake Wendover had his home. She wondered which one it was and knew that anyone who could afford such a place, could certainly afford very good nursing care if he needed it.

The foyer was warm and scented as Nuala stepped into the hotel. She looked about her as the attendant took her coat to the cloakroom and she went to tidy her hair in the pastel-coloured powder room. Thank goodness I followed Odinga's advice, she thought, seeing the racks of fur jackets and elegant casual coats, not unlike the one the girl now took from her. Her dress was comfortable and fitted in with the muted good taste of the hotel, yet managed to be young and pretty. She glanced round the bar, but there was no sign of Mattie. A glance at her watch told her that she was early and she wished she had the confidence to order a drink, but she sat on a green velvet chair at one end of the long room and watched the door.

The window by her side looked out on to the main drive, where several cars were parked, and a taxi came to deposit a family of four with enough luggage for a month. A car with a bright blonde girl and an older man who might be her employer stopped, the man obviously trying to impress the girl with him. A large imposing car like the one that Nuala had seen at the hospital gathering leaves, slid into a parking space. She forced herself to look away. It couldn't be the same one and it was high time she stopped seeing Blake Wendover's car whenever she saw a black limousine. It was enough to have the man in her thoughts all the time.

She looked up and saw a tall man striding to the entrance as Blake would once have done. Her throat tightened and she fumbled in her bag for a tissue, horrified that she might cry in public. She remembered that she was wearing eyeshadow and must not smudge it. Oh, Mattie, she thought. Do come soon before I panic. I wish I hadn't come here. It's not my kind of place at all. This is his place, the kind of hotel where Trudie would look about her without reserve and even dare to find fault, and of course the kind of hotel that must be familiar to Mattie. Anxiously, she looked towards the door again, willing Mattie to enter.

A man wearing dark glasses was coming towards her, as firmly as if he was on a ribbon attached to her table, or as if he could see her.

She put a hand to her throat. It couldn't be true. She had heard of the uncanny instincts of the blind, but nobody but Mattie knew she was in the hotel and even she could not know where Nuala was sitting. If he couldn't see her, it was a miracle of extra-sensory-perception; If he could see, it still made no sense—he had not seen her in hospital under circumstances that would have led him to remember what she was like. He knew the description that Trudie had given him, and now, perhaps he knew that, because Mattie had described it, she would wear a violet dress, but the girl with wide hazel eyes and frightened hands sat still while her handbag slid from her lap as he came near.

'I'm sorry if I kept you waiting,' said Blake Wendover.

'I'm early,' was all that she could say.

'What will you drink? Or shall we go straight in to eat? We can have wine with the meal, unless you have any rooted objection?' He bent down and touched her hand. 'Don't look so stricken. Am I no substitute for my mother?' The dark glasses were no longer opaque and at close quarters were not very dark at all, but as if the wearer had to have them in very strong light.

'You can see,' she said, in a low voice. Then, 'You can see!' as if accusing him of a dreadful subterfuge.

'Of course I can see? Didn't I tell you?'

'No you did not. And why couldn't Sister French think to mention a tiny unimportant matter like that, I wonder?' Her Irish temper flared as will the temper of a mother who sees her child escape falling under a bus and so shakes him in angry relief.

'I asked her to let me tell you and she thought I had done so,' he said. 'My mother was forbidden to discuss my condition in case Trudie found out and the wonderful security of the private wing did the rest. Nothing leaked out of my recovery until to-day.'

'Why today?'

'You were off duty and wouldn't hear immediately and I had to be sure that Trudie was out of the country before I announced that Mr Micheljon had made a perfect seal and the sympathetic condition of the other eye has cleared up. I have to wear these when I drive, and if the light is bright, but in four weeks I leave them off for good.

'I don't understand,' she said. 'Was it so important for Trudie not to know?'

'I nearly failed in that when I rang her brother, thinking she was well on her way to Geneva, but I had to be sure about many things and it was better that everyone thought I would never fully recover.'

'I still don't understand.'

'You'll feel better when you've been fed,' he said, kindly. 'Come on, they won't keep our table for ever.'

'How can you be so casual? Don't you know a miracle happened? And how did you know me when you never saw me before in your life?'

'You do go on, don't you? I had no idea what a chatterbox you could be,' he said, sternly, but she saw the gleam of mirth in his eyes.

'You only had Trudie's description of me and that wasn't very flattering, I'm sure.'

'It was not,' he said, with an Irish inflection.

'You're laughing at me,' she said. 'And what have you done with your mother? I was to meet her, or so I was given to understand.'

'I haven't done anything. She had to go away on business as soon as she knew I was all right, and I asked her to make this appointment before she went. I didn't want everyone at St Jude's to hear me making dates with members of staff. I thought you could do without rumours about us.'

Nuala looked at the menu that so far had been an unintelligible mass of words and tried to concentrate. So this was a polite gesture just to make her feel good, but not one to compromise him in any way. His deception was cruel and meaningless, a ploy to rid him of the woman who chased after him down all the ski runs of Switzerland. I'll keep my dignity, she thought and try to enjoy the last time I'll see him. She chose at random and saw his eyebrows shoot up.

'Are you that hungry?' he asked and she blushed when she discovered she had chosen two main courses. He suggested a light starter of avocado and prawns and she nodded, glad to leave the choice to him. He ordered white wine and, as she crumbled her bread roll, nervously, smiled with a sweetness that made her heart ache. 'I am sorry, you know. I can't tell you how sorry I am that I couldn't let you know I was going to be cured. I realise now that you must have suffered.'

'What makes you think that? I just like to be kept informed about the progress of my patients, or I fail to have, what do they call it in industry? Job satisfaction? It isn't important.' She spooned up the creamy avocado and thought how much she would have enjoyed it at any time but this. He regarded her thoughtfully. 'You still haven't told me how you knew it was me. Did the girl in the foyer tell you that there was an odd girl wandering about in here?'

'I have a confession to make,' he said. 'I could see you slightly the day you came to recovery with my clothes. You clutched my case like a refugee with no place to go,' he said, smiling. 'I could see through tiny slits they had left so that I had forward vision only.'

'I was not like that,' she said, and blushed. 'You couldn't have known it was me. I didn't speak as Sister told me just to leave the clothes and come away.' She stared at him, balefully. 'You couldn't match the girl to the voice.'

'You were wearing the shamrock,' he said. 'I knew it was you because only three of us wore it, and I know Sister French.'

Nuala looked down at the empty dish. She remembered standing at the foot of the bed with tears in her eyes. Had he seen her tears? or had he seen just a blur of a girl whose outline he would know again?

They finished their lamb cutlets and chose puddings from the trolley. She chose fruit salad and Blake had cherry pie with cream. 'No gateau,' she asked with a malicious smile.

'No gateau for a very long time. It reminds me too much of Switzerland. I crave a really good apple pie.'

'I make good pastry,' said Nuala. 'When I go back to Ireland, I shall bake a lot.'

The eyes behind the dark glasses lost some of their sparkle. 'You've decided to go back? Does that mean you will give up nursing?'

'I don't know.'

'Are you going for any particular reason, Nuala?' She told him about the house left to her by her grandmother. 'So you are a lady of means now?'

'Hardly that, but I hate to sell it. If I don't live there, it would be a cruel waste to have it empty for months on end.'

'It could be useful when you marry,' he said.

She shrugged. 'When I marry.'

'Your rather talkative nurse had a lot to say about your future plans in that direction,' he said. 'She was full of enthusiasm for the man of your choice and took it for granted that you would marry soon.' Nuala took another spoonful of fruit salad. 'Trudie was another one who told me all about it,' he said. 'Tell me, Nuala, have you set a date for your wedding?'

'I can't think why Miss l'Estrade should take it on herself to discuss my affairs,' said Nuala with dignity.

'She thought you might be gaining too much of my attention and approval,' he said.

'But that's silly. How could anyone compete with someone as beautiful as Trudie? I mean, it wasn't true,' she added, lamely. 'I suppose that now you are fit, you will be making such plans.' Hadn't Mattie told her that Blake was in love?

'With Trudie, no. I have never been in love with her, but I couldn't embarrass a lady.'

'She thought she was engaged to you,' said Nuala.

'She imagined that, as usual, she could have what she wanted and I wasn't asked,' he said. 'I've seen a lot of her because her brother is one of my best friends and, because of him, I tried to spare her feelings and convince her that the decision was hers to go away and leave me.'

'And I thought you were being noble, letting her go when you love her. You fraud!'

'I know. I was very sorry to see you looking so upset the day she went away after that unfortunate scene in the room.'

'You saw me then as well? You knew then that you would be all right. You are nothing but a liar, Mr Wendover!'

'I told no lies. I told Trudie that I would make no

further progress and would remain as I am for the forseeable future.'

'And as you said it, you knew you were cured?'

'I had to rest until the scar was firm, but there was no doubt in my mind that I would regain my full sight.'

'You are a cruel and devious man.'

'I'm sorry if you feel that. Let's go back to my apartment for coffee. I'm expecting a telephone call and should be there. Do you mind?'

Nuala remembered what Mattie had said. He was in love. The call would be from her and Nuala couldn't bear the thought of being there. 'I can go back to the hospital. I've taken enough of your time, Mr Wendover.'

'Don't you think it's time you called me Blake? We are friends, I hope.' He smiled. 'I can't come to Ireland to dance at your wedding if you call me Mr Wendover. What would the Irish think?'

'They'd think I showed you due respect,' she said.

'Get your coat,' he ordered. 'It's as well I brought a car. You have dear little feet, Nuala, but what silly shoes for this weather.'

She stalked off, sure that he was laughing at her. I always get treated like a child, she thought, when underneath, I want to be a woman. Her face flamed as she recalled her own naivety, but how was she to know any better when she thought he was blind? She had wasted her affection and sympathy on a man who now treated her reactions to his suffering as a joke. All her instincts told her to escape and she looked round the car park hoping to see another taxi looking for a fare after leaving passen-

gers at the hotel, but there was no taxi and the rain
was coming down in relentless sheets. She knew he
would think her even more of an idiot if she rushed
off through the rain in her thin grey shoes.

'Ready?' His hand under her elbow steered her
away from puddles and into the car. He brushed a
raindrop from her face as she sat beside him and her
heart was beating much too fast. How could she
forget this man when she had been so close to him?
How could she go on with her work as if nothing
had happened to change her whole outlook on life?

The car stopped outside a large house and Blake
took out a key. 'I have the ground floor and the next
one for my use,' he said. 'The flat at the top is an
office, a room for my secretary and a separate
apartment for my caretakers who look after the
place for me.'

Which adds up to the whole house being owned
by Blake Wendover, thought Nuala, with wonder.
The hall was panelled with glowing wood and in the
fireplace in the sitting-room, a clear fire burned,
although the house was heated with ducted air. He
helped her off with her coat. 'My turn to make the
coffee,' he said, and his smile nearly turned her
knees to jelly with its sweetness.

'I could do it if you'd show me where everything
is,' she said.

'Not this time.' She looked up, sharply. 'I hope
that you will come again, perhaps with Mattie
before you go back to Ireland, Nuala. She hopes to
see you again even if it is not with me, but I hope we
can arrange something that suits all of us.' He
walked away, leaving her gazing into the fire.
Could she bear to come here to take tea with

Mattie, sitting by his fire as if she belonged there
when her heart was breaking? But she knew that
any pride she might have had was ebbing away. She
would accept the crumbs of his attention even if
they were crumbs of gratitude and not of love. She
would come to meet Mattie, say all the right,
conventional things to him and tease him mildly
about his behaviour as a patient.

She sighed. Professional training was useful in
such circumstances. It might be quite easy, now
that she had surfaced from the first shock that he
had seen her as she was on duty, and hadn't been
completely repulsed by her lack of glamour. She
saw a log fall and bright sparks lit the goldy-brown
flecks in her eyes. Once or twice in the restaurant,
the eyes behind the dark glasses had glowed with
something other than polite attention. She forced
herself to believe it was an illusion, imagined because she couldn't read the true expression in his
eyes.

She moved restlessly and wondered if it was the
heat of the fire that made her cheeks glow. In the
car, his hand had lingered as he brushed away a
drop of rain on her cheek. There had been a tension
not entirely of her making. She sat higher, away
from the fire, on an easy chair made for a Victorian
lady with full skirts, knowing that it gave her dignity
with her back straight and firm. She felt more
confident than when she sat in a low-backed chair
from which she had difficulty in rising.

'Poised to escape?' he said, mildly. 'Are you
comfortable in that terrible chair?'

'Quite comfortable, thank you.'

He put the tray on the table by the settee and

poured coffee. There were tiny *petits fours* on one dish and brandy snaps on another. 'You'll have to come here to drink this,' he said. 'I *am* an invalid and I can't be expected to get up each time you want a *petit four*.'

'An invalid? That you are not, Blake Wendover.' She sat still, her colour high but eventually had to get up to take the cup offered to her. She walked across the room and he put the cup on the table again, moving slightly to make more room for her to sit beside him. She sat down, as far away from him as she could get, without falling off the rather spongy piece of furniture. She dared not look at him.

He stirred his coffee. 'Tell me all your news,' he said, in a conversational tone. 'How is Dermot?'

She choked on a brandy snap and put her cup down on the table. 'He's well, I think.'

'I wonder why Trudie was so insistent that you were going to marry him. The other nurse thought so, too. You know, the little nurse who gossips from morning till night and who I was afraid might tell Trudie that I was better if once she knew.'

'Well, you know there's no smoke without fire,' said Nuala. 'He came over to ask me,' she said. It was her only defence to make him think she might still marry Dermot.

'Smoke can obscure truth at times,' he said. 'Glamour and beauty of the conventional kind can hide many things. They can be the thick smoke that hides a mean and grasping nature.' She looked up, briefly, then looked away.

'You know that he is like that?'

'Not only Dermot. When my eyes were darkened, it was then that I saw the truth that needed no sight to see it. I had no idea how trying Trudie could be, even as a friend. Tell me,' he said, taking her hand. 'No ring? Do Irishmen not bother with engagement rings?'

'They do when a girl says yes,' she said.

'And you are still considering his offer?'

'It's a big step to take,' she said.

'But you've known him for years and yet you are still undecided. I hope it doesn't take such a time to make up your mind about everything.'

'Of course not, but I think that marriage should be for ever. I have to be sure.' She turned away and whispered, 'I couldn't bear to be hurt again.'

'I'm glad you feel like that,' he said. 'Isn't it good to find how much alike we are, Nuala? I could never marry a woman who had just a pretty face, even though I find beauty very attractive.' His hand raised her face and he saw her trembling lips. 'True beauty is in all the senses, Nuala. You are very beautiful.'

Her eyes filled with tears. The control she had so desperately sought broke in a wave of love. 'Blake,' she said, 'you mustn't tease me. I can't bear it.'

He kissed her and she opened her eyes and saw the man who already possessed her heart. His dark glasses had gone and in the smouldering depths of his eyes she saw tenderness, passion and a lasting love. 'May I dance at your wedding in Ireland, my love?' he said.

'We'll dance all night,' she said, with a catch in her voice.

'Not all night. We have to go on a honeymoon.'

'And where will that be?' she said, hoping that it

wouldn't be Switzerland. She couldn't take Switzerland just yet.

'You tell me. How far do we have to walk to get to the house by the sea?'

'Grandmother's house?'

He kissed her tenderly. 'Our second home.'

Doctor Nurse Romances

Amongst the intense emotional pressures of modern medical life, doctors and nurses often find romance. Read about their lives and loves in the other three Doctor Nurse titles available this month.

TREAD SOFTLY, NURSE
by Lynne Collins

'Avoid throwing yourself at a man – it's always a mistake.'
Why should the arrogant Mr Duffy care if Nurse Tiffany Kane ruins her reputation and loses her job because of a silly infatuation? For she loathes *him* with a startling intensity.

DR VENABLES' PRACTICE
by Anne Vinton

The position of Nurse-Receptionist in Dr Laurence Venables' Harley Street practice is viewed with mixed feelings by Staff Nurse Penny Hunt. For, despite his extreme good looks, the distinguished Dr Venables makes her hackles rise – even when he isn't trying!

ICE VENTURE NURSE
by Lydia Balmain

Against the advice of Dr Kurt Rothwell, Sarah Barford is appointed nurse on the exploration trawler, *Ice Venture.* Trying to prove she is every bit as capable as a male nurse is almost impossible while the difficult Dr Rothwell is intent on proving his point . . .

Mills & Boon
the rose of romance